HE'S ON TOP

HE'S ON TOP

EROTIC STORIES OF MALE DOMINANCE AND FEMALE SUBMISSION

EDITED BY
RACHEL KRAMER BUSSEL

CLEIS
PRESS

Published in the United States by Cleis Press Inc., P.O. Box 14697, San Francisco, California 94114.

ISBN-13: 978-1-57344-270-1

Printed in Canada.
Cover design: Scott Idleman
Cover photograph: Roman Kasperski
Text design: Frank Wiedemann
Cleis Press logo art: Juana Alicia
First Edition.
10 9 8 7 6 5 4 3 2 1

"Not Until Dawn" by N. T. Morley was originally published in *MASTER/slave*, edited by N. T. Morley (Venus Book Club, 2004). "Confession" by Gwen Masters was published at Cleansheets.com on May 24, 2006. "Incurable Romantic" by Lisabet Sarai was originally published in *Confessions: Admissions of Sexual Guilt*, edited by Sage Vivant and M. Christian (Thunder's Mouth Press, 2005). "Schoolgirl and Angel" by Thomas Roche first appeared in *The MILF Anthology*, edited by Cecilia Tan and Lori Perkins (Blue Moon Books, 2006).

Contents

INTRODUCTION: TENDER TOPS AND SENSUAL SADISM

Dominant men get a bad rap in our society, being lumped in with so many scary, dangerous examples of male lust gone awry that there's little space for the ones who, like James Spader's character in *Secretary*, simply get off on having a hot girl submit to their will. When I conceived of *He's on Top* and its companion volume, *She's on Top*, I wanted to pay homage to the power—physical, mental, and emotional—that goes into being a true top. Not one who's simply going through the motions, but one who cares about the context of their kinky actions.

I wanted to see creative kinksters devising scenes that would challenge their participants. I wanted to go beyond simple name-calling and into a place where power exchange matters, where the interaction between top and bottom could be treated with all the reverence and complexity it deserved. I wanted to show vanilla readers that S/M isn't all about whips and chains (though those can be plenty of fun, too), but also about mind games that truly fuck with your head. I wanted kinky readers to see themselves reflected in these pages, to feel that same thrill they do when a luscious bottom bends over, bows, offers their wrists to be bound, scurries to do their bidding. I wanted these stories to embody all that it means to be a top, whether a full-time one or an occasional visitor to dom(me)landia.

Perhaps not surprisingly, putting together *He's on Top* was altogether a more challenging prospect than assembling *She's on Top*. For one thing, though I've been a top *and* a bottom, I've never been a man, and I wanted this volume to do justice to dominant men in all their glory. For another, many of the submissions I received started out with some variation on the theme of "Get over here, bitch," betraying a sexism that was the complete opposite of the spirit of this book. I was dismayed to see that some people interpreted "man on top" as somehow condoning cruelty or meanness, because that's not what I consider to be sexy in any way.

Thankfully, the fabulous writers collected here, both male and female, show a more nuanced, and infinitely sexier, version of BDSM. They understand that erotic power play is not about taking power from someone, but rather about exchanging and exulting in power that's freely given. These tops get off on watching their women writhe, moan, and beg as they get spanked, teased, taunted, and tied up. They know what they like, and have found ways to incorporate it into their erotic scenes to enhance their pleasure, and that of their partners. One without the other simply cannot exist. These men need to play, need to top, need to control, just as much as their women need to submit, surrender, and obey. These powerful guys understand the true gift they're being given every time a woman offers herself up for their perusal or makes herself into an object for them to command and control.

Mike Kimera explores this phenomenon brilliantly in his tag-team topping story "Christmas with Suzy and Mary," in which his protagonist proclaims, "The first time I hit Mary, I was in a kind of trance. She was bent over a chair, naked, butt in the air, an improvised gag in her mouth, and she wanted me to hurt her.... It was as if I'd jumped off a cliff, and instead of falling, had discovered I could fly. I felt powerful and purposeful and connected to Mary more intimately than I would have thought possible." Exactly. Without Mary's wanting it, his joy would have dissipated.

It's this exquisite erotic thrill that you'll find time and again in this anthology, as masters, doms, tops, and other manly men find ways to make the women in their lives surrender not only their bodies, but some other part of themselves as well. Often these are strong-willed, powerful women, such as Kirsty in Lee Ash's "Boardroom Etiquette," who's torn between her innate submissive nature and her willful personality. Both collide as she tangles with her coworker in a feisty match between equals.

What surprised me is how proficient female authors are in the art of writing about male dominance. They rose to the occasion and produced stories that get deep inside the male mind. Some of the stories you'll read in *He's on Top,* such as Shanna Germains's "The Sun Is an Ordinary Star," powerfully capture the ways in which dominance and masculine identity intertwine. Her hero's struggle to express his love for his wife is challenged by a pair of nipple clamps, as well as by the idea that, for her, submission and masochism are a way out of the other kinds of pain she's experiencing. He feels guilty for wanting her in that stubbornly sadistic way he still does, and yet he cannot stop. "Although he tried to think of other things, his mind was all Stella, Stella in nipple clamps, her ass beneath the flat of his hand." Thankfully, he doesn't have to relinquish BDSM, and their dance of dominance and submission relieves both of them of some of the stress they each carry around.

Other female authors show us that these tops want to rocket their subs off into space, then soothe them back down to Earth.

There's a tender mercy to their sadism; being always on the lookout for her pleasure, they know it's the key to unlocking their own. As Donna George Storey writes in "Yes," "You can push her over the edge and catch her at the bottom, soft and safe in your arms. You can watch her dance and be inside her all at the same time, because you are the music she's dancing to now, faster and faster." As she explores a man offering his lover to a visiting friend, watching and overhearing, waiting to see what will happen, she gives a glimpse into a relationship charged with the intensity of two partners bent on exploring their deepest fantasies with one another, giving and taking, forging a life together that neither could achieve apart. It's this intimately twisted dance, where one step forward by the top necessitates a step back by the bottom, that flows through her tale. And in Lisabet Sarai's "Incurable Romantic," a top who from the outside might appear to be dominance incarnated lets us in on his own fears and doubts, offering up a touching vision that will make you question who's really got the other wrapped around their finger. Because even though these are tops' tales, the pleasure and needs of their bottoms are never far behind.

Please join me, and these authors, on the journey these men take to get to the top. While their paths are varied, they all share the desire to give equal parts pain and pleasure, to control even as their lust threatens to undo them, to master even as they become beholden to their wily, naughty, bratty, beautiful bottoms. Seeing how they get there—and what they do once they arrive—is enough to leave me breathless, and I hope these stories do the same for you.

Rachel Kramer Bussel
New York City
August 2006

NOT UNTIL DAWN

N. T. Morley

Tonight is the night you're going to make me wait all night. All night for your cock. All night for my come. All night for what I need, most of all: you inside me.

You take me out to a late movie, a foreign film everyone's been raving about. It's filled with sex, the steamy tale of multiple seductions. I don't see much of the movie, though, just the beautiful press of flesh as the European actors writhe together in bed. We sit in the back row of the near-empty theater and make out, my hand resting casually in your lap, stroking your hard cock through your pants. Your tongue explores my mouth, your teeth nipping at my lips. You slip your hand under my dress and finger fuck me, first one finger, then two. But you don't let me come, even though I'm very close. You can tell when I'm close, and you make me wait, letting me cool down before you start to finger me again. I beg you to let me come, but you won't. "You're going to wait," you tell me. "You're going to wait all night."

"Please," I whimper, and you slip your hand out from under

my dress and bring it to my lips, making me lick it clean. The taste is sharp, tangy, delicious; it sends a warm surge through me. I never would have tasted pussy before the night you made me yours. Never, ever. I'd never even dreamed about it. Now, when you put your fingers in my mouth, I suck on them hungrily. My cunt is yours, and so it tastes beautiful to me.

You kiss me again, deeply, and my hand gently rubs your cock as your mouth takes me more aggressively this time. You finger me again, and I'm dying from need. I start to unfasten your belt and unzip your pants. I lower my face into your lap—I've got to have you. I've got to have your cock.

You grasp my hair and pull me back up, pressing me into the creaking theater seat. Your mouth is on mine again, forcing my lips wide open, taking my tongue and possessing it.

"All night," you tell me. "You're going to wait all night."

"Please," I beg you, but you shake your head.

"Zip it up," you say, and I draw your zipper back up and awkwardly buckle your belt.

I look into your eyes and you kiss me again, your hand sliding once more up my dress and fingering me as I beg you to stop. "I can't take it anymore," I breathe, but you know that I can. And even if I couldn't, you wouldn't care. You finger me until I'm right on the edge, until just the slightest touch of my thighs together would make me come harder than I've ever come before.

"All night," you tell me as your hand eases up my shirt and begins to play with my nipples. "You're going to wait all night."

We leave the theater after the movie and drive to a nice restaurant you've selected—one that's open late. As we eat, your foot stretches out and rests casually between mine, checking the distance between them, making sure I'm keeping my legs spread. Not too far—not far enough to draw attention. Just far enough to let me know that my pussy is exposed, that you can see it if you look under the table. You drop your fork several times, I notice. Each time, I feel the heat of your gaze on me, shooting right up my dress. It makes me want you, right here. And the feel of your foot against mine, ensuring that I don't close my legs, drives me crazy. You're just letting me know that you own me. Letting me know that my legs are yours, to spread as you see fit.

You take me for a long drive through the beautiful hills above town, the city lights spread out below us glimmering like diamonds. You reach over and slide your hand up my dress, casually, never taking your eyes off the road. Your middle finger penetrates me, careless, almost disinterested. I moan. "Moan as loud as you want," you tell me. "You're going to wait all night." You finger me until you hear my moans change, feel my hips bucking against you, and then you pull away and casually change gears, downshifting into second. We've reached the summit.

Before you let me out of the car, you make me lick you clean, slipping your middle finger into my mouth. I suck on it, the taste pulsing through me and making my tortured clit hurt bad. "Please," I beg.

"Please what?"

"Please," I beg you. "I need to come."

"Not until dawn," you say.

I slide up against you, my hand on your belt buckle.

"Please," I whisper. "Please let me suck it."

You shake your head. "Not until dawn," you repeat.

We get out of the car. You drape your jacket over my shoulders and lead me to the railing that overlooks the city, the lights so brilliant they blind me. You push me hard against the railing, and I feel like I'm hanging over the city. Your arms go around me and you cradle me tight, crushing me against you. Your cock rubs me through my dress, against my ass. I want it so badly I moan. I whimper. I grind my ass against you. You kiss the back of my neck and make me shiver. You slip your hand up my dress and start to rub my clit. You put your middle finger into me and start to finger fuck me again. I shudder and whimper, begging. *No. Please. Please stop. No. I can't stand it.* My nipples are hard against your jacket. You tease those, too, your hand up my shirt and moving from one nipple to the other to ensure that they both stay hard. Your feet are planted firmly between mine, making sure I keep my legs spread. Your cock remains motionless as you let me grind my ass against it. The city lights swim in front of me. My breath comes in great, gasping sobs.

"It would be so easy," I moan. "Just pull my dress up and ..."

"Not until dawn," you tell me once more, and start to finger fuck me harder, making me lean against the railing and moan at the top of my lungs.

You drive me to a bar for a nightcap. It's close to last call, and we find a booth near the back where almost no one can see us. We both slide into one seat. You lean against me and sneak your hand up my dress again, but this time you don't touch me. I relax into the soft cushions of the booth, my legs spread, and beg you. "Please. Please. Please." But you won't touch me. You just let your fingers hover there, inches from my pussy, and it's worse torture than I've ever felt. Within moments I'm on the edge of orgasm again, and you've never even touched me. The pink champagne tastes sickly sweet and it makes my stomach tingle. The smoke of the bar swirls around me and I lose all sense of direction. Am I awake or asleep?

You kiss me, and I know I'm asleep. And dreaming. A nightmare. A nightmare of want, of need, of desire. You slip your hand into my mouth and I would swear I can taste my cunt. I lick you eagerly. I beg you for more. I run my hand up the swell of your cock and whimper for what I need.

"Please," I whisper. "Let me suck your cock. Right here. Let me suck it, right here in the bar."

You shake your head and kiss me. "Not until dawn."

You drive me back to our apartment and lead me up the stairs. Once inside, you grab me and push me hard against the wall right by the door, before you've even closed it. I moan as I melt into your grasp. You grind your cock against my front and I reach down to cup it. I try to push my hand down your pants as you kiss me. You seize my wrist and pull it away.

Leaning firmly against me, you undress me right there. You slip my dress over my shoulder and let it shimmy down my body, revealing me. I'm not wearing panties or a bra. My small breasts feel so tender against the rough wool of your jacket. My nipples ache as if they're going to explode. I long to be pressed against your body, wriggling up and down as you savage my mouth with yours. "Please," I beg you. "Please let me suck it?"

You pull me off the wall and guide me toward the bedroom, one hand on my shoulder and the other on my hip. I can hardly walk, I'm so turned on. I can scarcely stand, my cunt hurts so much. I stumble into the bedroom and you push me across the bed, forcing my legs open wide, this time with your hands. I see what you're doing and the terror grips me. No. No, you can't. You can't do this to me. It's too much. I can't stand it. No, please.

But what I say is simply: "Please."

Your mouth descends between my legs.

From the first touch of your hot tongue on my aching clit, I know I'm going to come. You know it, too, and it's only that first touch you let me have. Your breath tickles me, sizzling my flesh. Your tongue undulates an inch from my clit. I beg you, tears streaming down my face. I need it. I have to have it. But you make me lie there, spread wide, until you know my orgasm has subsided. Then, cruelly, you begin to eat my pussy.

I sprawl across the bed, clawing the sheets viciously. Moaning "No, no, no, no, no," unable to stand it. About to die. About to disintegrate. About to explode.

Your tongue swirls around my clit in exactly the way that makes me come—then stops. You tease my pussy lips. You lick down to my entrance, slipping the tip of your tongue in. You lick around my clit, blow on it, tease it with your breath. You do everything but make me come.

"Please," I beg you.

I feel your fingers inside me again, and my moan comes louder than ever. My back arches. I push my cunt down onto you, taking as many of your fingers as you'll give me. You finger me until I'm on the edge again. I've lost all perspective. I've lost all sense of time. I know I'm going to die if I don't come. I know you're going to kill me by torturing me like this.

"Please," I beg. "I can't take it. Oh God, I can't take it ..."

And then my wide-open, glassy eyes see it: The first hint of light through the window. I want to tell you it's dawn. I want to ask you to fuck me. I want to beg you to make me come. But I can't. I can't say anything but "Please, please ... no, no, no, no, no." I'm so far beyond speech I can barely even manage that. My body writhes under you as you start to eat my pussy again.

And I'm on the edge again. You stop.

But this time you stand up, towering over me at the foot of the bed. I watch you, eyes wide, as you take off your clothes. All of them. Your cock stands out, straight and hard. I would give anything to touch it. Anything at all to taste it. Everything I have to feel it inside me, thrusting. Fucking me. Taking me. Making me come.

You slide on top of me, naked. My body presses up against yours, seeking. My legs spread still wider. My ass lifts off the bed.

"Please," I say as the streams of light tear through the blinds and savage me.

I come the second I feel your cockhead penetrate me. I come a second time as I feel your shaft sliding into me. I come a third time as you grind your hips hard against me, forcing your cock in and out against my desperate flesh. I come a fourth time as I thrust my body up against yours, wailing, sobbing, taking each hard thrust you give me and begging for more. My arms and legs are slack; only my hips and my cunt exist. And my mouth, wailing in hunger. More, more, more, more, more.

The fifth and final time I come is when I realize you're about to come, too. Hours of pent-up need. Your cock filled with semen, about to flood my pussy. That drives me over the edge one final time, and as the sunlight bathes us I rise onto you, lifting you wholly off the bed until nothing is touching but your knees. Then your body tightens, and you come—deep, deep inside me, deeper than you've ever been before.

"Not until dawn," you promised, and you made me wait. "Not until dawn," you told me, and you gave it to me. I came hard at dawn, harder than I've ever come before. More times than I've ever come. My arms come into being again and I wrap them around you—my legs, too. I clutch you close as you heave a great sigh of exhaustion.

"Thank you," I whisper, but you're already fading. The sun feels cool on my flesh, and your breath on my face feels warm. I close my eyes and vanish into your heat.

INCURABLE ROMANTIC

Lisabet Sarai

She is, without a doubt, the perfect slave.

I should know. I've trained half a dozen slaves over the last twenty years, and played with perhaps half a hundred more.

In Minneapolis? you ask, incredulous. The law-abiding, church-going, vanilla-flavored heartland?

Why would I lie? I'm past the point where I have to prove myself. We have our own kinky little community here, invisible to those who don't want to see, obvious to the initiates who know the signs.

Like Ilsa's collar. If you weren't one of us, and you happened to notice it, you might think it's one of those choker necklaces so popular with the Britney Spears set. It's braided black leather, strung with tiny diamonds. You might expect a matching diamond stud piercing her navel.

If you truly paid attention, though, you might recognize something unusual in the way Ilsa wears it. She holds her head exceptionally high, her back straight, her graceful neck extended,

showing the collar off like a badge of honor. Which of course it
is, my gift to her on her completion of one year in my service. In
truth, though, wearing it is her gift to me, a tangible and public
statement of her total devotion.

She never removes it. The candlelight makes it sparkle now,
as I gaze on her naked, bound beauty. Her wrists are roped together and fastened to the hook in the ceiling. A few red-gold
locks have escaped from her barrette and trail down her back,
contrasting with the darker red of the stripes my whip has carved
in her tender flesh. Her creamy skin is flushed and damp with
sweat. I kneel behind her and use my tongue to gather a salty
drop that has run down her spine, just as it is about to disappear
into the shadows between her swelling buttcheeks.

Ilsa shivers in delight at my touch. I reward her by pulling
her open and lapping at her anus. She is still loose and slick with
lube and my come. She cannot help responding, pushing her
hips back to invite me deeper into her dark recess. I draw away
and land a rousing slap on one buttock. "Didn't I tell you to be
still?" I growl.

We both understand that my anger is feigned. "Yes, Master,"
she murmurs. "I'm sorry. When you touch me, it's so difficult."

"A well-trained slave knows how to control herself." I don't
tell her, of course, that she is perfect. "Clearly, you need more
punishment. Turn around."

On tiptoe, the spreader bar between her ankles making her
awkward, she manages to maneuver her body to face me. Her
eyes are cast down, those long sooty lashes of hers (so different from her spun-copper hair) making spiky shadows on her
cheeks. Her lips are parted, her breath comes fast and shallow.

I intend to apply my whip to those luscious breasts of her,
gleaming and still unmarked in the light of the candles. Instead,
I find myself kissing her, sharing the funky flavors that I just

sampled from her butthole. She opens to me, not only her mouth but her whole self, allowing me to feast on her until I am sated. She keeps nothing back.

Candlelight and kisses. I may be a nasty old dom, but I'm still an incurable romantic.

It's true that I've never known surrender as complete as what Ilsa offers. I find it a bit scary. She tells me that she will do anything for me, and I almost believe her. I'm sure that she has limits; everyone has limits, that's S/M 101. But I haven't found them yet.

I've used paddles and floggers of every description, clamps and clothespins, electricity and chili oil. I've staked her out, naked and in full view of the world, on the balcony of my condo in January. This is in Minnesota, remember. After ten minutes, her ivory skin turned blue. She never complained, never used her safeword. I hastened to bring her inside, wrap her in blankets and make her drink her hot tea and brandy. The clear light of adoration in her eyes never wavered. I was the one who felt chastened.

I've shared her at play parties, watching as my friends buggered and beat her. Afterward, she was more tender and attentive than ever. I'll never forget the night that I invited two rising stars in our community, Master Shark and Mistress Valentine, to come over and try her. They were far rougher on her than I could ever be. After an enema and a caning, being fisted by Shark and pissed on by Valentine, she was bruised and exhausted, but apparently in a state of bliss.

"You know you could always stop them, Ilsa," I told her later. "They know your safeword, and they would honor it."

"But, Master," she murmured dreamily, on the edge of consciousness, "I wanted to please you."

She does please me, of course. Sometimes I can't believe my good fortune, to have won the devotion of this angel/slave when she could have chosen a younger, more handsome, more energetic dom.

Often, though, I realize that there is something wrong in our relationship, something missing. Thinking about her brings on an unpleasant anxiety, vague but annoying.

I'm thinking about her now, as I sit sipping Starbucks cappuccino and trying to read Murakami. Could any person truly be so pliant and submissive? What kind of childhood did she have, to make her this way? When I asked, she told me that her upbringing had been "normal," unexceptional. Did I believe her? Why would she choose a master so much older than she? Old enough to be her father? There must be some secret here, some story she won't, or perhaps can't, share, even with me.

All at once, my thoughts are rudely interrupted. Something slams into my chair from behind. My coffee leaps out of the cup and onto my lap. My cock is scalded, even through my trousers and undershorts. Anger rises in me as I turn to confront the culprit.

"What do you think you're doing? You should be more careful!" I don't need to shout. My voice naturally carries the authority of long years of dominance.

"Oh, I'm so sorry!" My first impressions are youth, plumpness, a certain disheveled quality that is not entirely unappealing. "Are you hurt?" She notices the coffee stain spreading over my crotch. "Oh, dear! I am really such a klutz!"

Her eyes are a warm brown behind wire-rimmed glasses. As she gazes in dismay at the mess in my lap, I find, to my chagrin, that my half-boiled penis is hardening in response to her attention.

She doesn't miss this sign. There's still concern in her voice, but I catch a hint of laughter as well. "I really apologize. I'll pay for the dry-cleaning, of course."

"No need," I say, more gruffly than I intend. I pull my chair closer to the wrought iron cafe table, trying to hide my erection. "My housekeeper will get the stain out."

An image flashes involuntarily through my mind: Ilsa on her knees, nude except for her collar, scrubbing my pants on an old-fashioned washboard. Meanwhile I tower over her, jerking off into her hair. This picture does nothing to reduce my arousal. I think that's the key to being a great dominant—a kinky imagination that is always at work, even at the most inappropriate moments.

"Oh, please, let me do something to make it up to you! I'll buy you another coffee." Before I can stop her, she's at the counter conferring with the barrista. I pretend to read, but actually I'm surveying her, trying unsuccessfully for a dispassionate evaluation.

She carries more weight than is fashionable, but it's all curves. Her soft olive sweater and jeans emphasize this. She has straight brown hair that she has tried to confine in a ponytail; wisps escape all over to hang untidily around her face. She moves with a determined energy, solid and confident. I contrast her headlong progress, as she stumbles among the tables balancing two cups, with Ilsa's fragile grace. There's no comparison. Still, I find, I want her.

She seats herself across from me. "Double cappuccino with skim milk, both cinnamon and chocolate, right?" She barely gives me the chance to nod my assent. "I guess you're a regular here, too. I'm surprised I haven't seen you before."

"I'm pretty inconspicuous," I comment lamely, knowing that with my height and dominant presence, this is not at all true.

"Hardly!" she says with a laugh. "Anyway, I'm glad to meet you now, though I'm sorry to have damaged you and your pants in the process." She tries to steal a glance under the table, to gauge my current state of tumescence. I have foiled her by transferring my book to my lap.

"I'm Kate," she says holding out her hand. "And you are ...?"

"Riordan," I say, finally, when it's clear that I can't avoid answering.

"What an unusual name!"

"It's Celtic," I say. "Traditional in my family."

"Well, it's very romantic." Her smile is infectious. "What do you do, Riordan?"

"Officially, I'm retired. Early retirement," I hasten to add. "I was CEO for an industrial equipment distributor. Now I do a bit of this and a bit of that. Play the stock market. Do guest lectures for MBA programs. Write." Train slaves, I think privately. I try to imagine Kate shackled and on her knees and fail utterly.

"I noticed you were reading Murakami and wondered if you were a writer. He's not exactly in the best-seller category." She sighs and stretches her arms over her head, causing her sweater to bulge delightfully, and my cock to follow suit. "I'm working on a novel, myself. In my spare time, of course. My day job is writing advertising copy."

"Well, at least it's writing," I say. This girl confuses me, with her aggressive friendliness.

"Yeah, well ... it's not much fun, but it pays the rent." She has an idea; I can literally see it light up her face. "Speaking of apartments, why don't you come over to mine for dinner some time soon?" She places her hand casually on my thigh. "I'm an excellent cook; all my friends say so."

She can see my hesitation. She turns up the pressure. "Please, Riordan, let me make up for my clumsiness by cooking you a nice dinner. How about tomorrow night?"

It's strange to have a woman call me by my name instead of "Master." Once again, I have a sense of disorientation. I know I should refuse, for my own sake as well as for Ilsa's. But somehow, I can't. Or at least, I don't.

"All right. What time?"

"How about seven?" She tears a sheet out of her notebook and scribbles something in a round, flowing script. "Here's my address and phone number."

"Uh, thanks." Where did my usual eloquence go?

Kate glances at her watch and stands up so suddenly that she nearly overturns her own coffee. "Oh, God, I've got to go! I'm really late. Is there anything you don't eat?"

I shake my head, speechless in the face of her energy.

"Great! Well, I'll see you tomorrow, then." She grabs my hand and squeezes it enthusiastically. "Thanks for being such a good sport, Riordan."

My hand and my cock are both throbbing in the wake of her whirlwind departure. I'm puzzled by my own reactions. My well-honed instincts tell me that Kate has no interest in kinky games. She's young, fresh, horny, and 100 percent vanilla. Whereas I have had dominant fantasies since I was in grade school. I really can't understand why the prospect of ordinary, unadorned sex, without any paraphernalia or power exchange, suddenly seems so intoxicating.

Ilsa is waiting for me at the door when I return home. She is completely charming in her French maid costume: translucent black organdy top, frilly lace apron, and bare buttocks. And her collar, of course.

"Good evening, Master. Would you like a cocktail before dinner?"

"Scotch on the rocks. Please." I feel awkward with my sweet slave in the aftermath of my encounter with Kate. "But I think we will go out for dinner tonight. Wear the green silk sheath. Without any underwear."

"Of course." Ilsa is trying to smother her smile and remain serious and respectful. She loves it when I take her out and show her off. She is already imagining the clinging softness of the silk against her bare skin.

The sting of my palm on her exposed behind brings her out of her reverie. "What about my drink, slave? Do I have to teach you how to provide such a simple service?"

"No, of course not, Master. Right away, sir."

She hurries off, swaying on her spiked heels. I admire the reddening image of my hand on her white flesh as she disappears into the kitchen. Perfection indeed.

The next evening, I chain Ilsa to the foot of our bed. "I have to go out," I tell her, as I hand her the water bottle and the chamber pot. "I have some business. I may be quite late."

Why am I lying to her? We both know that I am the Master. I am free to do as I wish. She has chosen to accept that. If I want to see another woman, isn't that my prerogative?

I realize that if I were going to a play party tonight, or to help break in another dom's slave, I'd be telling Ilsa the truth.

I have no illusions about tonight's dinner engagement. I can see very clearly what Kate wants, can see it long before she opens the door wearing a tight red jersey dress that showcases her ample cleavage and plump, freckled thighs.

We don't even get past the second glass of wine. With dizzying speed, Kate propels me into her bedroom and sucks me into a hot, wet kiss. She tears off my clothes with such abandon that I worry, briefly, about damage. Then she sits me on the bed and does a slow, delicious strip tease in front of me.

She slips one strap off her shoulder and I catch a glimpse of the black lace cradling her lush breasts. The other strap slides down and they're revealed in all their glory. No padding needed here. In fact, the lace is so delicate that her rigid nipples visibly distort it.

Next she gradually raises her hem to just below her pubis.

"Want more?" she whispers. My swollen cock bobs in my lap. I suppress the urge to grab her, rip her dress open and ravage her, and simply nod.

She pulls the dress over her head, displaying her black satin thong. Her breasts rise and tighten at the motion. My cock aches. I can't take much more of this.

Kate seems be losing patience, too. She slips the thong down her thighs and kicks it away, then unhooks the brassiere in front. Twin globes of ripe flesh spill out. I lick my lips, my mouth suddenly flooded with saliva. With a half smile, Kate takes a step closer and feeds me her abundant tits, one at a time.

Before I can understand how it happens, I am on my back, with Kate astride me, riding me hard. She's wild, bucking and squirming, all her monumental energy focused on that spot where our bodies join. She rubs at her clit with one hand, pinches her nipple with the other. I grab her hips and arch up into her, trying to give her what she needs to push her over the edge.

I'm enjoying myself, of course, but I am somehow removed from the scene. I watch our bodies writhing with the same sense of detachment that I feel observing a couple fucking at a play party. I am simultaneously aroused and distant. I'm as hard as I have ever been, but it feels as though I am a long way from coming.

Her orgasm is a noisy cataclysm that, to my surprise, sweeps me away with it.

Afterward, Kate feeds me quiche and salad in bed, washed down with two bottles of white wine. Then she snuggles up to me, trapping me in her arms, feathering my cheeks with kisses. "Thank you, Riordan," she sighs, half asleep already. "That was wonderful. You're a fabulous lover."

I don't respond. What can I say? *If you think that was good, you should try me when I've got a flogger and some nipple clamps?*

Kate sleeps. I don't. I'm turning the whole experience over in my head, wondering what I have done, and why. I think about Ilsa, waiting for me in chains, and tears prick my eyes.

Near dawn, Kate rolls over, releasing me from her embrace. I tiptoe around the bedroom, gathering and donning my scattered clothes. I notice my shirt is missing two buttons, and that Kate snores.

I should kiss her goodbye, I know, but I'm afraid that I'll wake her. So I sneak out of her apartment like a thief, ashamed and guilty that I am abandoning her.

I haven't smoked in fifteen years, but now I buy a pack of cigarettes at a 7-11 and prowl the empty sidewalks of the city, lighting one after another, shivering in the October chill.

I've already forgotten Kate; it's Ilsa that I'm worried about now. In some strange way, it seems, I've betrayed her trust. She asks nothing more from me than to be her Master, to train her and mold her, to guide her toward more complete submission. To perfect her.

And what do I do? I leave her alone while I chase some juicy vanilla morsel who just wants me for my hard and willing cock.

I'm lazy, that's the plain truth of it. But that's not all. I'm afraid. I tell myself that I can't fathom Ilsa's limits, but have I really tried? Have I accepted the fact that I might need to give her more, push her harder, go deeper with her than I've ever gone with a slave?

Perhaps it's really my limits that need to be expanded. There are things I could do, implements I could use, that I've never tried. To be honest, they make me uncomfortable. If this is what Ilsa requires, though, can I deny her? I understand, suddenly, that it is not only Ilsa who needs to be perfected.

She's asleep, curled up on the carpet, when I tiptoe into the bedroom. A stray beam of early morning sunlight filters through the drapes and gilds her coppery curls. She looks like an angel, but what angel ever displayed the fading pink marks of a caning on her unblemished skin?

A pang of guilt and regret lances through me, as excruciating as physical pain. I don't deserve her. I should set her free.

I am about to turn away and slink out of the room, when she stirs.

"Master," she says, not trying to hide her smile. "You're home." She raises herself onto her knees, thighs spread, wrists clasped at the small of her back, as I taught her. She dares to look up at me. "I missed you."

I need to be stern with her, I remind myself. I need to offer her extremes of pleasure and pain that far surpass anything we've yet experienced together. I must be willing to bring her to the point where she trusts me enough to utter her safeword without fearing my displeasure. No matter what it takes.

I must be fierce and implacable, cruel and merciless, immune to any doubt or fear, in order to be the dom that she needs.

Incurable romantic that I am, I can only kneel beside her and take her in my arms.

SEIZING MONICA

Debra Hyde

I t's simple, really. Her struggle makes me hard. Doesn't matter what she's doing. If Monica struggles, my dick reacts and I want to fuck her. Is something primal at work within me? Perhaps. I know my mind is civilized, always telling me that because she has consented to this, it's all right. And, yes, my heart softens at the thought of her sanctioning what I do to her. But my dick doesn't react like my heart or my mind. When Monica thrashes about, it rages stiff and mean.

I suppose there's something primitive about my dominant urges. It's like the mighty hunter, the human predator, suddenly catching the scent of a woman in heat. The smell of cunt, telling him, in a language more ancient than words, that sex is at hand, that it's worth throwing away the spear of the hunt to spear something else entirely. That a woman can squirm like quarry is all that the primitive part of my brain needs to see.

The thinking man in me isn't subjugated by this, though. He schemes and fantasizes. He's the one who decides whether I'll do an elaborate scene of bondage and whips or employ a simple but severe over-the-knee spanking. He's the one who plans whether Monica will suffer humiliation or objectification or, should he hit on a particularly devilish idea, both. He's the one who provokes the primitive within and makes it happen.

But it's Monica who makes it possible. Make no mistake; none of this is possible without her. My prowess is impotent without her. She comes to me and thrives on what I provide, willing to walk into my clutches and take whatever I decide she'll receive. When she kneels before me and offers herself up to me, she is both angel and sacrificial lamb. When I take her, I wonder if this is how a god must feel before his minions.

Last night was one such example. Monica came to me, as commanded. She stood before me naked, the curves of her body gentle in their beauty. Yet the pleasure of seeing her was no simple admiration. I surged with lust when I saw her nipples perched hard atop the swell of her breasts, when I saw her clit peeking out invitingly from the slit of her cunt. It was a survey that made my cock twitch in anticipation, and it would compel me to act.

Monica is irresistible, and the hunter in me could easily throw her down and take her at first sight. But the thinking man forbids it. He prefers to toy with her, to tease and test and torment her long before pouncing. Foreplay must be savored. Haste makes waste.

I approached her, wrapped my hand around her long hair, and pulled her head back. The strain of my pull shivered through her as I kissed her. I could feel it even though I held her almost an arm's length away. Her body tensed, afraid to move lest the pull reach her scalp. She was captive to my grip and it made our kiss all the more heated.

She wanted to swoon, to collapse and surrender. I sensed it as

I played about, plying my tongue and encouraging her to buckle to my kiss. But each time she relaxed a mere iota, she felt her scalp burn and she jerked back into that tense, rigid posture.

Her demeanor drove me to taunt her. It's a natural response, I think, to exploit an opening, a weakness. It's like coaxing a fish to take the bait. Or knowing how a poker hand is destined to play out. You see it and seize it. And I had my way of seizing Monica.

One hand held her, the other one wandered lower. I caressed her thighs, taunting her with the possibility of further touch, further exploration, but waited. It's a slow process, this teasing, and one must let its effects mount. I waited until Monica moaned and arched toward me, but even when she made this move, I delayed the maneuver she longed for. Instead, I squeezed the flesh of her thigh, and my grasp told her that I'd take her in chunks if I could. Monica trembled against this touch, so close to the collapse I wanted to claim from her.

Close enough that I abandoned my clenching grip and brought my fingers to her clit. I brushed them over her clit, that little bulge of pleasure, suggesting that more touch would follow. Again, she moaned. She ached for it now.

I rounded her clit briefly with my index finger, circling it, then rubbing just enough to entice her. Instantly, she surrendered and withered in my grasp. Fiercely, I pressed her to me and held her against me, but wandered lower still until I reached her hole. Slickness greeted me and I imagined the look of her cunt lips gleaming. I promised myself I'd have it soon enough.

But more taunting, more teasing first—my scenario called for it—and so I wiped my finger along her slit, wetting it before returning it to Monica's clit.

She quivered again when my touch met her and, this time, I let her think she had earned an early reward from me.

"Like this?" I asked. "I do. Because you please me."

I coaxed her into believing I was sincere in pleasuring her. I goaded her with whispered words and the swirl of a sure touch. Both circled her, enticing her with sentiments and sensation, but when she stiffened against my touch, when her groan sounded deep, I knew she'd grown too near, too quickly. I pulled from her, suddenly, and interrupted the spiral that would take her to orgasm. She gasped and cried out. I had thwarted her.

Yes, I wanted to pleasure her. I was sincere in that pledge. But pleasure comes in more than one form, and it's not orgasm I wanted her to feel. I wanted her to experience the thrill of denial, an excruciating pleasure unto itself.

"Not yet," I decided. "I don't want you to come just yet."

I let go of her hair and took her by the nipple, a particularly cruel delight. In our play, it's the same as being taken by the arm. I led her across the room and Monica followed closely, knowing that if she slacked so much as half a step off my stride, she'd feel the pull of my pinch.

The distance was short, just a few yards, from one end of my den to the other. There, I took a blindfold from a desk drawer and tied it around her face. She was not to see what came next. That, I could not allow.

I left Monica standing there, blindfolded and anticipatory, and went about preparing for what would be this scene's penultimate struggle. She could, however, listen to me move about and although she had, in the past, guessed what I brought to fruition, she had never encountered exactly what I had in mind this time. Guessing would not be easy.

She heard things being fetched from the drawer and my moving across the floor. She knew the room and could figure out that I was near my desk chair. She heard duct tape rip, but the sound was not clue enough to tell her more. She heard me

strip myself of my shirt—perhaps the only clue she could sur-
mise—which hinted that this next scene might be laborious for
me. When I grabbed her nipple again, she knew she was about
to face her fate. I pulled her toward it.

She was perplexed when she heard the click of the lube bottle
opening. Confused, she frowned, knowing full well that I was
not about to fuck her, knowing she had not suffered enough to
merit it. She trembled when she felt my hand at her cunt lips and
lube on my fingers. She issued a second gasp when she realized I
wasn't going to penetrate her.

"Spread your legs," I told her. "Back up a step."

She backed into the chair—hard enough to grunt at the impact—and I maneuvered her into place.

Right over a thick, nine-inch dildo.

Monica moaned when she felt its head at her lips, when I
worked it into her. I had her put her hands on top of her head.
Then, I put this scene into play.

"Fuck it," I demanded.

It was not an easy penetration for Monica. Mounted on the
arm of the chair, the dildo was unforgiving and the chair itself
required her to straddle it at a slightly awkward position. Still,
she sank down on it and slowly worked herself up and down.
The deeper she took it, the more difficult it became, and when
she staggered slightly against the chair, I knew it was not a comfortable penetration. She struggled to find a tolerable position,
one where she could fuck without feeling pierced. But she did
achieve a pace, one I could work with.

Monica had no idea that her strife was about to escalate.

I stood, waiting, watching, looking for just the right moment,
and the first time she slacked off her pace, I struck.

The sting of my signal whip landed just above her navel.
Monica jolted and cried out.

"Faster. Come on, fuck that thing."

Monica picked up her pace. Again, I stood watch; again, she soon gave reason for another strike of the whip and, in short order, a cycle of defeat came into play. Each time she took the whip, Monica sped up, but each time she did so, her endurance waned sooner. No matter how well she complied, Monica could not long suffer the tempo I required of her. Her body quaked with growing fatigue and she bore a look of raw misery.

I kept at her with the whip. I wanted marks—bright bee-stings and long stripes, intensely red when flesh is tender, near abrasions where bone and flesh meet too closely. These, Monica soon sported. Her belly, her thighs, her breasts, even around her cunt, these marks she bore. And all the while, she fucked that dildo.

Her strength finally diminishing, Monica leaned forward from the waist and made her breasts a whole new target for me. Aiming the whip at their underside, I struck and her breasts quivered deliciously. This became my whip's finale and I struck swiftly, often, demanding the last of Monica's compliance and energy. I demanded that she fuck faster, take the whip harder, and expend herself for the sake of my dick.

Rigid, I ached. The marks, her strife, her unfailing if fading compliance, all made me ripe. I dropped the whip and freed my hard dick. I pulled Monica from the dildo and pushed her to the floor. I grabbed her wrists and forced them above her head. Braced against them, I forced her thighs apart and plunged into her.

It was like fucking a cunt primed by others—open, wet, yet tight enough to make your dick throb—and I wasted no time in taking her. Thrusting, I pierced her deeply and used her roughly.

Beneath me, Monica lay there, exhausted and slack jawed and loving every minute of it. Fucking is the big payoff for her, the prize she earns by enduring her master's sexual schemes, and, this time, sheer, endorphin-ridden bliss came with Monica's reward.

I rose up and surveyed my work. The sight of marks gracing her body aroused me so much that I trembled and lurched closer to orgasm. I didn't hold back. I pounded her, slammed her. Monica was a hole for my need, a convenience for me to use, a means to my end, and when I felt that surge, I let loose. I pummeled her as I came. Growling and grunting like a rutting, wild beast, I came, filling her with my success. And, success achieved, coming complete, I collapsed.

I took my respite there, on Monica. I rested, my mind small with flickers of delightful thoughts—the marks, her strife, the feel of her cunt when I took her, the objectifying thoughts that made me come; I revisited them all in a long, lingering daydream. This is why I dominate her, why I command her.

And when I felt her hand on my head, when her fingers lightly stroked my hair, I knew Monica relished submitting to it.

This, too, is why I dominate her.

CONFESSION

Gwen Masters

Clarice didn't love him anymore.

The knowledge came to her like a calculus problem finally solved. Something that made no sense whatsoever until the answer was right there in black and white, and then of *course* that was the way it was, why didn't she see it before?

At the moment of revelation she was looking down at Max, watching him watch her, his hands playing across her breasts in the same way they had for the last twenty years. Suddenly he was only the man she was married to, the guy who paid the bills, the man who liked his steaks rare and his vodka neat. He wasn't the love of her life anymore.

Was it a sin to fuck someone she didn't love? She supposed it was. But she closed her eyes and made him come anyway.

She knew her performance was convincing. In all the time they had been married, he never noticed when she faked it.

At confession the following week she sat primly in the little cubicle. Father Brian sat on the other side of the tarnished grate.

Though she could see his profile, he carefully kept his face turned from her. She confessed her sins one by one and then said calmly, "I have slept with someone I don't love."

"Slept with?" the priest said, confused. She clarified. His eyes widened and, though his profile did not change, his tone did.

"Have you spoken with your husband about the fact that you do not love him any longer?"

"No, Father."

She could barely see him through the grate that separated them, but she could see enough to read his displeasure clearly. The priest shook his head slightly, a frown on his face. It made his collar look even tighter around his throat. "The Lord blessed your marriage. Honesty between you and your husband is vital. This is what the Lord wants."

Clarice shifted in her chair and bit her lip, thinking. "But if I tell him that, it will destroy him, Father. Maybe I just need to find someone to fill the void, someone who will take care of my needs and still allow me to be a good wife."

"An unfaithful wife is not a good wife," the priest admonished.

"Divorce is not allowed," she whispered, and a long sigh came from the other side of the confessional. She ignored it, forgot about confessing her sins, and started talking about making new ones. "Divorce isn't allowed but infidelity isn't considered such a sin in the Church. Why is that? Why is infidelity over-looked but divorce is enough for excommunication?"

"That's a good question," Father Brian admitted. "But that doesn't change what we have here, does it? It doesn't change the fact that you need to do something in this marriage to which you have committed yourself. We offer counseling sessions for this. There is nothing wrong with admitting there is a problem with the marriage. There is something wrong with dealing with it by sinful means."

"Forgive me for the sin of considering it," she whispered.

"Yes," the priest returned, but Clarice was sure she heard a note of doubt. He gave her a remarkably light penance, and Clarice found herself in her car minutes later, looking at the rosary in her hand and feeling even more lost than before.

That night, Clarice looked at Max over the dinner table. She watched him chew the green beans, watched him dip the bread into the pool of butter on the potatoes, watched him cut through the steak. Watched the blood sluice out of it onto the plate. Her stomach turned.

"Do you still love me?" Clarice asked, and Max dropped his fork. It clattered against the plate. A dollop of mashed potatoes landed on her clean tablecloth.

"Where did that come from?" he asked.

"Things change," she whispered.

"They do?"

"Yes." Wetness seeped around the mashed potatoes on the tablecloth, widening the stain.

"Do *you* still love *me*?" he asked.

The question was her opening, her chance at freedom. But, like a prisoner who has known nothing but the walls of a fortress for a little too long, she hesitated instead of dashing for the wide-open gate.

"I don't know," she said.

"You don't *know*?"

She looked up at him. Her husband's face wasn't a mask of pain or confusion, like she had expected. It held a touch of anger, and something else. Relief?

Relief?

She stared at him dumbly, unable to speak. Max shoved his chair back from the table so hard that he upset his wine. It sloshed over the tablecloth, red on cream, and Clarice groaned.

She would never get that stain out. Somewhere deep in her mind, it occurred to her that she was more upset over the stain than over the certainty that her marriage was picking up momentum on a downhill slide at this very moment.

She looked up to see empty air where Max had been. She heard him tramping down the hallway, heading toward their bedroom.

"Max!" Clarice was gripped with sudden terror. What had she done? What was she thinking? So what if she didn't love him anymore? He was her husband and she had a responsibility to him, she had taken vows, right in front of God and everybody, she had worn that gold ring until it had made a permanent groove in her flesh. If some doctor took X-rays of her hand he would probably find a groove in her very *bone*. She was his for better or for worse, and this just happened to be worse.

What had she done?

Max was standing in the bedroom, looking down at the floor. He appeared very interested in the designs on the carpet. It was as if he had forgotten his mission and purpose. Clarice touched his back and he flinched.

"I've known for a long time there was something wrong," he said. "I didn't know it was this bad. I know we've been stifled and unhappy for years."

She heard the "we."

"You've been unhappy too?" she said. "You never said …"

"Neither did you."

"I don't know what I need," she whispered. "Sometimes when we're making love I think I feel the things I should feel but then …"

"When was the last time you came with me?" he asked bluntly. Clarice was too stunned to answer. Max turned to look at her. His eyes were wide and clear and there was something in them she had never seen before.

"Last night," she whispered.

His eyes narrowed. "Liar," he said, and the word was long, drawn out into a vicious tease.

"Last year," she corrected.

Max blinked once. "I've been having an affair," he said.

Clarice drew her hand away from him as if she had been shocked with electricity. She stumbled back against the open door, and the edge of it cut into her back. She tasted blood in her mouth. She had bitten her tongue. An affair? Max?

"But you never try anything new in bed," she hissed. "She obviously hasn't taught you much."

In two steps Max had a grip on Clarice's wrist. She tugged hard to free herself and he used brute strength to pull her out of the doorway. He flung her onto the bed. She bounced once, then turned onto her back and scrambled away from him, her feet bunching up the covers and shoving the pillows from their careful places. Max grabbed her ankle and hauled her back down. With the other hand he yanked on the top of her blouse.

The buttons flew and ticked on the hardwood floor.

"What are you doing?" she screeched.

"I think what you need is the same thing I need," Max said. He hadn't even broken a sweat. He removed his glasses and dropped them to the floor, and this surprised Clarice enough that she stopped moving. Had Max ever been so careless?

"Are you going to get on your knees, Clarice, or should I make you do it?"

"I'm not going to suck you off," she spat out, and tried to kick her ankle free. He twisted ever so slightly and Clarice gasped when a tiny sliver of pain shot through her leg.

"No, you're not," he clarified. "Not yet."

"You're crazy!" she almost screamed.

Max yanked hard on her bra. The elastic stretched against

her flesh but there wasn't much give, and she felt the snaps go, two little hitches against her back and then he had access to what he wanted. He took one nipple in his hand and pinched. Hard.

"Ow!" Clarice hollered. Max glared at her.

"Tell me you don't want it like this, Clarice. Tell me that and I'll stop." He twisted her nipple just enough to make her cry out again. "I fucking *dare* you, Clarice."

Her mouth dropped open. She had never heard Max curse before. "What did you say?" she asked.

"I said: I fucking *dare* you to tell me to fucking *stop*, Clarice."

He let go of her ankle. When he reached for the snap of her jeans, she was too stunned to stop him. They were halfway down her legs before she remembered that her husband had just admitted to an affair, that she didn't love him, and that they were supposed to be fighting, not fucking.

But she was more turned on than she had been in years.

She kicked the jeans off. Max eyed her warily, expecting some sort of trick. Clarice arched into his hands and he obliged by squeezing her breasts hard. Still looking at her, he scraped his teeth over one nipple before he bit down.

The pain flashed through her and she writhed under him. His hips pressed against her crotch. She was dripping wet and what was in his pants was hard as a rock.

"I want you," she gasped.

Max licked a trail down her body. She listened to the sound of his zipper opening and his pants hitting the floor, even as his tongue found her clit. For the first time since they had been married, Max wasn't gentle. He nibbled and licked and sucked until Clarice felt as though her whole body would come apart at the seams.

That was before he slipped a finger up her ass.

Clarice arched off the bed, all thought gone. She screamed when she came.

Another finger joining the first brought her back down to earth. This new invasion hurt a little, but the pain was eclipsed by the thrill and the sheer goodness of it. She ground down on his hand while he bit softly along the inside of her thighs.

"Do you want me to fuck you there?" he asked. He was just as breathless as she was.

"No," she immediately said, and Max pushed a third finger inside her. She yelped and tried to move away but his other hand held her steady. She found herself pushing hard against him and chanting "no" at the same time, a mantra of uncertainty.

"I'm going to fuck your ass, Clarice," he told her. "I'm going to fuck you there and I'm going to come deep inside you. Because I've decided that I like dirty little sluts and it's high time I had one of my very own, don't you think?"

Clarice was stunned. A wave of shame washed over her. Her face turned a brilliant red. Her heart pounded.

"I'm not a slut," she protested weakly.

"Not yet, but you want to be, don't you?"

She didn't answer. She just bucked up against his hand. When Max told her to get on her knees she did it meekly, but she could hardly breathe for how fast her heart was racing.

"Did you go to confession today?" he asked her, seemingly out of the blue. He had the lube from the bedside drawer, the bottle she had bought when menopause brought about all sorts of awful changes in her body. This time she was so wet he almost didn't need it. She moaned and arched her back at the sensation of the cold liquid sliding across her puckered rim. He was going in *there* ...

"Yes," she whispered.

"Did you confess all your sins, Clarice?"

"Yes."

"I want you to confess them to me. I want you to tell me all the bad things you have done. I want you to tell me how you fucked me even while you didn't love me, and I want you to tell me how you faked those orgasms, and I want you to tell me how bad you want this cock in your ass."

Clarice started to tremble. The head of her husband's cock pressed hard against her back door and she tensed up, suddenly afraid.

"Confess," he whispered.

"I fucked a man I didn't love," she said, and as she did, she felt him push harder. Now there was a slow, burning sensation between her cheeks, but she found it was more pleasant than anything else. "I faked orgasms for a long time. I acted like the good wife when I really wasn't."

"Tell me more."

"I played with myself while my husband was at work," she said, and Max paused in surprise. Clarice bit down hard on her lip while the burning spread, filling her whole center, making her whimper in protest.

"I'm not going to stop," he said, "Because I know you don't want me to. Confess."

"When I played with myself I pretended that I was fucking someone else. I pretended my husband was tied to the chair in the bedroom and made to watch while someone else made me come over and over and over."

Max pushed harder. Clarice cried out with the sudden flash of pain. Almost immediately the pleasure took over and then there was a dull roaring in her ears, the sound of her own blood pumping furiously. Her clit throbbed.

"Do you like being fucked up the ass, Clarice? Do you like

feeling like a slut? Only sluts do that, you know. No good Catholic girl would dream of letting a man sodomize her. This makes you a godless heathen, doesn't it? It makes you a *slut,* Clarice."

With that, her husband shoved his cock to the hilt, buried himself between her cheeks, and ground down hard against her. It hurt like hell but, God help her, she wanted it. She cried out and thrashed under him, not sure if she really wanted to get away, knowing damn good and well he wouldn't let her anyway.

"Are you going to confess this to Father Brian?" Max panted. "Are you going to confess that you let that man you don't love fuck you up the ass? You're just sinning all *over* the goddamn place, aren't you, you fucking *bitch?*"

Max rubbed her clit with every word, a rhythm of curses and caresses that sent Clarice over the edge before he even started to truly fuck her, and she was coming hard before he pulled back and thrust in hard again. Before he started taking his own pleasure, she was screaming and clawing at the sheets.

Max didn't stop. She begged, she warned him she was too sensitive, the pleas coming out in an almost childish whine. He laughed against her back and kept right on doing what he was doing, and now he was sawing in and out of her ass, the lube making it easy but not gentle. She bucked up into him and in response he slammed down so hard that her breath left her in one long thrust.

He was cursing at her, calling her names like *whore* and *cumslut* and *cocksucking bitch.* She cried and screamed and her body heaved hard when she came, hard enough that she almost threw him off, and that was what it took to send him over the edge.

Max hollered when he came. He had never done that before. Clarice lay under him when it was over, her wrists gripped by his hands. He wasn't letting go of her, and he was buried deep inside her, even though he was going soft and small.

"I guess she did teach you new tricks," Clarice said after a while.

"There is no one else," he said. "I lied. I wanted to see if it would faze you."

Clarice tried to move away from him, but he held her easily, as if she were weightless.

"That's not fair," she spat.

"It's not fair that you don't love me anymore," he told her.

"Maybe I do."

"Maybe you equate love with lust, Clarice. As long as I'm fucking you like a cheap whore, everything looks different, doesn't it?"

His cock was getting hard. Clarice wriggled against it, to help him along. Soon she was on her knees again and he was fucking her hard, bottoming out every now and then and making her cry out in surprise. She buried her face in the pillow and pushed back against him, spread her legs wider, begged him for things she never would have asked for even an hour before.

"Confess some more," he ordered, and she did.

YES

Donna George Storey

The first time you see her, she's dancing with another guy. She's a good dancer, which means what she's basically doing is fucking out there on the dance floor. But she's not fucking him. Her body is moving all on its own, her hips thrusting into the air, her back rippling like silk, sucking the music up through the floor. She *is* the music. You can't take your eyes away from her ass and that bare band of skin above her jeans, shimmering with a fine film of sweat.

She turns and sees you staring.

You don't believe in love at first sight or auras or telepathy or any of that hippie-dippy shit, but at that instant a voice—not yours, but a woman's voice, and how the hell that got inside your head you'll never know—it whispers to you.

Yes.

Later you run into her by the metal tub where they're keeping microbrews on ice. She smiles. You take the opportunity to talk a little, make her laugh, get her phone number. She asks you to walk her to her car. The neighborhood's a little scary at this time of night, she says. As a reward for doing your Boy Scout duty, she lets you kiss her, long and hard, against the door of her Mini Cooper.

It's all so smooth and easy, you even start to think parties aren't so bad after all. Or maybe all those years you spent guarding the keg and stumbling home shit-faced drunk and alone because all the smooth-talking assholes got to the pretty girls first was just practice for this night, the one time you got it right.

The sex starts out great, and you have a feeling it's only going to get better.

It does. Each time, you learn something new. How she gets all hot and squirmy when you stroke the soft crease of her elbow with your fingertip. How she almost sobs when you push her knees up to her chest and go in deep, but then afterward she strokes her belly tenderly and tells you how good it feels to be sore there, like you're still inside her.

Then there's the time she asks you to come on her face. She's shy about it at first, mumbling into your shoulder about a fantasy she's had for a long time, but she'll understand if you don't want to try it.

Of course, you do.

As you straddle her chest and take your cock in your hand, it feels like something you've wanted, too, since before you can remember. It makes you rock hard to see her spread out beneath you, a meadow of smooth neck and cheeks and forehead, waiting for the rain. She's playing with herself as she watches you, with a look that's horny and curious and scared all at the same time. Her face is bright pink, and you can smell the seashore scent of her and hear that beautiful squish-squish of finger on sopping cunt. You time your strokes to hers and it's as if you're touching her and she's touching you. She seems to know when you're about to shoot your wad, because she closes her eyes and tilts her head back like a kid playing in a summer storm. When the first party streamer of come pelts her cheek, she sucks in her breath, then lets out a whimper with each new spurt. When you're done, she's a mess—beads of spunk in her hair, a shiny little puddle in the hollow above her chin.

She's still playing with herself and you reach down and start smearing the slick, soapy stuff all over her cheeks and lips. You give her nipples a coating, too, plus a pinch for good measure, causing her to arch and quiver. Then you start to feed her, spreading your spunk over her lips so she can lick it off, drop by drop. She tells you afterward that she loves the taste of your semen when she's turned on. She says it's like rolling around on a newly mown lawn, licking a dish of vanilla crème pudding that she snuck from the kitchen while it was still warm. Sure, her clothes are getting stained and her mom's gonna be mad that she's eaten dessert before dinner, but it's all so slick and creamy and deliciously naughty that she doesn't care.

You love it, too. The way she moans and sucks your finger like a cock when she comes. The way she opens herself to you, a little more each time.

You think how a new woman is like a pack of baseball cards. You tear open the wrapper, your whole body aching with the hope that maybe this is finally the one with the 1952 Topps Mickey Mantle Rookie Card waiting inside. But time after time, all you get are commons, hardly worth tossing in the drawer.

Now you look down and see her face, all shiny with your spunk. Her eyes are shining, too. You remember the chicks who winced at the mere mention of swallowing, who wouldn't even go down on you at all, and you see before you old Mickey in mint condition, holding that yellow bat over his shoulder as he gazes heavenward into a golden future. And you wouldn't trade this for all the money in the world.

The next time, her little surprise for you is to bake cookies, not from a mix, but special ones with white chocolate and raspberries and fancy liqueur. She says white, sweet, creamy things make her think of you.

You pretend to read the paper while she stirs up the batter and hums like some TV mom from the '50s. But she's not wearing an apron and pearls. You can see her nipples through her shirt and she has on the same jeans she had on the night you met, with a wide leather belt that makes you think of a slave girl you saw in a history book in school. Back then you wanted to do all kinds of nasty things to the girl in the picture, things you didn't have a name for.

You know what to call them now.

She waves you over, scoops up a swirl of batter on her finger, and licks it off slowly with the pointy tip of her tongue. She offers you a fingerful and you take it in your mouth. It's sweet—all butter and sugar and a healthy dash of booze—but that's not what makes you dizzy. It's the taste of her underneath, her flesh and her spit, which has the same faintly musky taste as her pussy. She told you once she smells different to herself, tastes different, too, since she met you. As if you've marked her.

That's the flavor you're searching for on her skin.

You think of taking her right here, lifting her up on the counter. Or bending her over the kitchen table, perhaps, doggy-style. But that little voice, the one you've learned to listen to, whispers again.

Wait.

So you pull away and slap her ass and say, "No more fun until you clean up these dirty dishes."

She pouts, but her eyes twinkle, and she gets right to work, humming her happy homemaker tune.

You walk to your bedroom. Already the plan is taking shape. You remember a story she told about her college boyfriend who begged and begged her to let him fuck her ass until she gave in, but it was lousy. He was too rough and it hurt and he was a real wuss about the mess afterward. She'd never done it since and wasn't sure she ever wanted to again.

In your book, if a guy begs a woman to let you fuck her ass, he should at least be a gentleman about it. You promise yourself you won't be like him.

You won't beg.

You open the drawer where you keep your condoms—plain, lubricated, flavored, for her pleasure—pick out a plain one, get the bottle of lube, and tuck them in your jeans' pocket.

She's bending over to put the last mixing bowl in the dishwasher—she really does have a beautiful ass—and sure enough, the place is spic and span. You come up behind her and wrap her in your arms. She sighs and starts to turn around. That's when you squeeze her hard enough to hold her in place.

"Put your hands on the counter and bend forward," you say. Your voice comes out firm but kind, part drill sergeant, part favorite uncle.

She snorts. "What?"

"You heard what I said. Are you going to be a good girl? Or do you want to hear what happens to bad girls who don't do as they're told?"

She giggles, but leans forward anyway. It won't be long before you'll have her making other noises.

You pull her shirt up over her breasts, glad you don't have to struggle with a bra this time. As you flick her nipples, you enjoy the silky sway of her flesh, ripe fruit dangling from a tree.

"Can you feel it in your pussy when I touch you here?"

"Yes." Her voice comes out tight and small.

"Is it making you wet?"

"Yes."

"I want to check. I hope you're not being a bad girl and telling me a lie."

She shakes her head.

You feel for her zipper, then yank her jeans and underwear down to her knees. You slide your hand between her legs. She wasn't lying. You play with her for a while, to feel the lips swell and her clit stand out hard like a little diamond.

"You are wet. Very wet. Too bad. It's such a waste."

She freezes, mid-moan. She doesn't say it, but you feel the question in her body.

That's when you take out the lube and pop open the top. You squeeze a few drops on your finger and smooth it along the valley of her ass.

"Don't," she cries, lurching away, but she's hobbled by her jeans and only manages to fall against the counter.

You hold her and hush her and tell her it's okay. Your fingers leave a trail of lube on her chest. "I don't want you to be afraid. Just focus on the sensations in your body right now. Do you think you can do that for me?"

She whimpers, but you know she's back with you because she leans forward to offer her ass again.

"We're going to take this slow since it's only your second time. I understand the first time wasn't so pleasant for you." All the while you're stroking her soft crevice very gently, then circling around the puckered entrance. "Tell me. Is this pleasant?"

She lets out an "ah" from deep in her belly. Her shoulders are heaving. You move your other hand back on clit duty. She's drenched down there.

"Push your asshole open for me. That's right. You do want this, don't you? You want me to fuck you in the ass."

Her little cry and the gush of her juices in your hand is answer enough, but you wait for the word, the sweet sibilance of it: *Yesss*.

You've gone in the back door before, but never like this, so carefully, like a sacrament. You pour out more lube. You anoint her with it and she opens, little by little. You slide a finger in and leave it there until she softens even more. All the while you keep tap-tapping her clit until she's shaking and panting and begging *you* to do it, then you roll on the condom, oil up, and knock lightly against the entrance.

She gasps, but it slides in easy once you get the head of your cock through the doorjamb. Later she tells you she's never felt so full, as if your cock was pressing all the way up into her skull.

"Try to move now," you say, low and soft in her ear. "Nice and slow. That's a good girl. You like it, don't you? You like the things I tell you to do."

She's in the zone now, beyond words. Her back is flushed and her head nods—*yes, yes, yes*—each time she thrusts back onto you.

You work her clit faster as her ring of muscle grips and glides up and down your cock. It's tight and good, but it's not like her pussy. Beyond that sweet rubber band at the opening, there is nothing. It makes you understand fisting—a weird gay thing you tried not to think much about before—but you understand now, because you want to be so deep inside her that you can nestle right up against her beating heart, but for now her pretty pink cock ring will have to fill that hunger. That and her voice in your head—*oh, God, you're fucking my ass, you're fucking my ass and it's good, oh, it's good*—and when she comes you really feel her spasms, milking you, squeezing you, and then you come, thrusting freely, hurting her maybe, but she's crying out, "Yes, yes, yes" and you know it's okay.

In the beginning you don't really plan any of it. Sometimes you only take advantage of a lucky set of circumstances. Like the night your old friend, Sean, stays over on his way back from a year at his company's Asia office. She offers to make dinner and you say yes because you like showing her off to your friends.

She bakes her special dessert again. You both call them "fuck-her-ass cookies" now, although she offers them to Sean as "raspberry surprise bars." When she goes off to get the coffee, Sean follows her with his eyes, as if he's still hungry.

"Do you realize I haven't had any action in almost a year? Nothing. I barely even talked to a woman. It was too depressing to pay for it. Oh man, it's been harsh. But you seem to have a pretty good thing going here."

You have to agree. She's perfect, just like that old saying—a lady in the living room, a whore in the bedroom. And sometimes the other way around, too.

It's then you get your next idea.

You pour him a little more brandy. You want him to be drunk, to think only with his dick. Since you met her, you don't drink much. You don't need numbness, it's sensation you crave, so clear and sharp it cuts into your flesh. Your dick is still important, sure, but sometimes it's your head that throbs with a tight ache, filled to bursting with dark, nasty longings. All you have to do is touch her, even look at her, and suddenly it's not trapped inside you anymore.

And so, after the fuck-her-ass cookies are eaten, you suggest some after dinner games.

The two of them frown and you know what they're thinking: Poker? Charades? Truth or dare?

What you have in mind is a little of all three.

"This game is called 'Secret Desires' and the lady always goes first," you explain as you pull the long chiffon scarf from your pocket with a magician's flourish. Sean looks clueless, but she blushes because she knows you use that scarf for one thing—to tie her up sometimes when you have sex.

You walk behind the sofa and look down at her. Her chest rises and falls in quick, shallow breaths. She leans her head back and meets your gaze, her eyes so big and wet and open that you could fall right into them, but you don't. Not yet. You make the scarf into a blindfold, knot it tightly around her eyes, and go sit in the recliner, leaving the two of them alone on the sofa.

Sean blinks stupidly, but there's no hiding that bulge in his pants. She is every man's dream sitting there, a scarf over her eyes, chest heaving, red lips moist and slightly parted.

"I'll tell you a little secret about my girlfriend, Sean, old buddy. She likes to show off. You should see her when we go to parties. She's practically spilling out of her shirt, and her jeans ride so low you get an eyeful of cleavage there, too. I don't know why she looks so prim and proper tonight. Let's let Sean see the real you, sweetie. Why don't you take off your blouse for him?"

She sits there, without moving, for the longest five seconds of your life.

You realize you're holding your breath. Even after all these months, you can never be totally sure you've gotten it right. You lead her to the edge of the cliff and give her that nudge, but she decides if she'll fly or fall. And wherever she goes, she takes you there with her.

Slowly, very slowly, her hand moves to the first button. You let out a sigh of relief and shift in the chair to adjust your boner.

She inches her blouse over her shoulders and pulls her arms from the sleeves. At your command, she takes off her bra, too, and sets it carefully beside her on the sofa. Eye candy's the word for her now. Her breasts are so pretty and tasty-looking, the aureole like disks of raspberry candy on her creamy skin.

"Why don't you show Sean what you like to do to your nipples when you're alone and feeling in the mood."

"Jesus," Sean murmurs.

She's being a good girl, doing exactly what you ask, rubbing her palms in slow circles over her breasts, twisting the stiffened tips between her fingers. It's not an act, either. Her chest is flushed and she's squirming and sighing.

"This is great, honey. Sean is really getting a better sense of you as a person," you say. "But I don't think he understands yet how much this is turning you on. Why don't you take off your pants and show our guest how wet your pussy is, too."

She winces under the blindfold and flushes a brighter shade of pink. But a second later she's shimmying out of her pants and underwear.

"Spread your legs," you say.

She obeys.

From where you're sitting, you can see her pink folds glistening with moisture.

Sean's eyes bulge. The cords stand out in his neck.

"Spread your legs a little more," you say. "That's right, let's get a good stretch. Now I want you to play with yourself. That's the part you like best, isn't it? Showing guys how horny you are?"

She lets out a little "oh" of shame and desire. Her hand moves slowly, as if she's dragging it through water, to nestle between her legs. Will she really do anything you ask? Part of you wants to stop now, send Sean off to bed with his fist and his dreams, but that voice fills your head again.

More. I want more.

"Yes, you've gotten our guest quite worked up with your

show, you horny little slut. I'll bet he wouldn't mind at all if you bent over and sucked his cock now. After all, that would only be polite."

She nods, dream-like, and moves closer to him, groping her way like a blind person.

"Kneel between his legs," you tell her.

She crouches and fumbles for his zipper. Sean snaps out of zombie mode to help her pull his pants down. His cock springs free. He's big, but not so big you have anything to worry about.

She doesn't seem to need directions anymore, because right away she starts licking his shaft with the flat of her tongue, quick, teasing little laps. Then she tickles the sweet spot beneath his swollen cock head with the tip of her tongue. He groans and paws her hair.

You're enjoying the view, the way her jaw muscles bulge and her cheeks hollow out when she takes him between her lips. She's definitely making an effort to do her best. You wonder if her eyes are closed under the scarf and if she's pretending that she's someone else. Or that he's someone else. You wonder if it's turning her on as much as it is you.

Sean is going crazy, humping up into her mouth, his face all twisted up with lust, and finally he gets the words out that have probably been on his mind for some time. "Hey, is it okay if I fuck her?"

"Absolutely, but remember, we're still playing Secret Desire so you'll use up your turn." You laugh, tossing him a condom.

Then you add, "But no anal, okay?" You want to keep that part of her for yourself.

"Yeah, sure, no problem," Sean mumbles. He's not going to press his luck.

You wait long enough to see what he's going to do. He lays

her out on the sofa and gets on top. She grunts softly when he enters her, then she turns her head toward you, just like the night you met. And just like that night, you sense the connection, through the scarf, through the hot, damp air of the room. She feels you watching and that's the only thing that matters—she tells you later this is exactly what was going through her mind.

Sure, Sean is the one pumping away on top of her and kneading her breast like bread dough, but he's doing it for his own pleasure. He isn't thinking of her.

That's the difference. You're always thinking of her.

You silently thank your dear friend Sean for being such a boring, predictable fuck as you get up and walk out of the room. No need to stay for the finish. By which you mean his finish, not hers.

Because, of course, you've saved your Secret Desire for last.

You go to your bedroom, undress, put on your robe, brush your teeth, take a piss, and lie down on your bed to get ready for your turn. Voices drift from the living room. Oddly enough, they sound friendly, like a real couple in the afterglow. She laughs. Your cock stiffens—you'd lost some of your hard-on while you got ready for bed—and you realize you're angry, too. You gave that bastard permission to fuck her, not talk to her, and you're tempted to call to her to get her ass in here right away. But you wait, your skin getting hotter and your cock harder, until she comes into the bedroom. The scarf is gone and she's dressed, but her expression is naked with excitement.

You know she's saved the best part for you.

First you tell her to lock the door. You don't want Sean nosing around for an extra pillow. He's taken enough of your hospitality for tonight.

She strips and joins you on the bed, pressing her wet crotch against your thigh like a little dog in heat.

"Did you like my game? Did it make you hot?" you ask, in that deep, smooth voice she likes.

She nods into your shoulder.

"Did you come for him?"

She pauses, as if she's wondering what the right answer is. But of course, there is no right answer.

She shakes her head.

"I'm disappointed in you," you lie. "You've been very rude to our guest." You lift her on top of you. She plants her knees on the bed and lowers herself right onto you. No condom, only skin against skin, your cock nestled in the warm, wet glove of her bare pussy. "The next time I give you to someone, I want you to come for him. Do you understand?"

She nods, grinding her crotch against your belly, desperately, as if she's afraid you'll tell her to stop before she reaches her climax. But you won't. Not this time.

"Do you promise? I want to hear you say it." Of course you're not sure there'll be a next time. There are other places you want to take her, new places where no one's ever been.

She's thrusting now, jerking her hips the way she does when she's close.

"Yes, I promise," she whispers.

"I was right, wasn't I? You are a show-off. You liked playing with your tits and masturbating for him. You liked making him hard." You spank her, slow and steady. With her cheeks spread in a straddle, you can land every few slaps on her sensitive crack. She makes a low, animal sound and pushes her ass out to receive the next blow.

"Yes."

She says your words are as good as your hands or tongue or cock at turning her on. It turns you on, too, to open her with your voice and slip inside her head. It's like wandering through a forest in the nighttime with huge stars winking in the trees like jewels.

"You liked fucking him, too. You liked it because I told you to do it. You'll do anything for me, won't you?"

Your chest swells with the possibility of it, because you can do anything together. You can push her over the edge and catch her at the bottom, soft and safe in your arms. You can watch her dance and be inside her all at the same time, because you are the music she's dancing to now, faster and faster.

She cries out a response, but you know it's the answer to another question, the one that matters more than anything. Because it's the sweetest sound a man can hear, a woman you love coming around your cock, moaning, sobbing, sighing, and whispering that one magic word.

Yes.

IN CONTROL

M. Christian

We met in the dark corner of an Internet chatroom. SLUT-SLAVE, a nubile profile full of in-the-know vernacular with damned good typing skills, and MASTER017, my digital persona. We didn't really meet there, of course, but that's where we first started to talk. The dance was slow, at first. I've heard other doms say that they don't like it slow, sedate, careful—they'd rather snap their fingers and have them drop to their knees. Me? I like the dance, the approach, the "chat" in chatroom. Besides, I've had a few of my own snaps, the eager young slaves with sparkles in their eyes and not a clue between the ears. Give me someone who knows what they're getting into. It's better, after all, to be wanted by someone who wants the best, as opposed to someone who just wants.

So we danced, we chatted, SLUTSLAVE and I—or at least that cyberspace mask I wore. Finally, after many a midnight typing, she complained with a sideways smile [;-)] that she was looking for something where more than her wrists got a workout.

Like I said: step one, two, three, turn, step one, two, three. Careful moves in this courtship dance. No snap from me. I made her sing for her supper, pushing her along, not making it easy for her. "Do you know what you're asking for, slave?" I asked, clicking and clacking on my keyboard.

She did the same, and the dance changed its tempo: "Yes, Master. I do."

We made a date to get together the next weekend.

A knock on the door. Normally, even when it's expected, it can be jarring. Fist on wood. Bang, bang, bang! But not that night. I opened it. "Welcome."

I had a picture, of course, and the flesh was just like it, though filled out in three-dimensional reality. Unlike the door, seeing her jarred me, but not unpleasantly.

"Thanks," she said with a smile, walking in. I closed the door behind her. Full bodied, curved, somewhere between too young and too old, tight and firm from exercise. Eyes gleaming with sharpness, mouth parted just so with anticipation. Curly dark hair, her skin a Mediterranean patina.

We didn't have to say much, most of our negotiations having been done in emails back and forth. I knew she couldn't stay on her feet for too long (plantar fasciitis), and didn't like metal restraints or canes—all of it. But her list of yeses was longer than her list of nos.

"Stand there," I said, pointing to the center of my wool rug. My room looked odd, with all the furniture pushed back, piled up: spare chairs on my big oak table, ottoman tucked underneath. The room was only the rug, a coarse wool bull's-eye, and my favorite plush wingback.

"Yes, sir," she said, the grin never leaving her lips, as she walked to the center.

"Stop." She did, turning slowly to face me. Her breasts were big, wide. Not a girl's, a woman's. Twin peaks on cotton fabric. No bra, as ordered. I reached out to one of the points, circled it slowly with a stiff finger. The smile stayed, but her breathing deepened, sped up. "Did I tell you what to call me?"

"No—" she hissed, trying to swallow a scream, as I pinched her nipple, hard. One of my nos concerned sound. My apartment had thin walls.

"Call me 'Master,'" I said, low and mean, grumbling and growling, as I pinched even more.

"Yes ... M-Master," she said, with a delightful stammer against the pain.

I released the pressure. "Pain is your punishment. It will be frequent. Pleasure is your reward. It will be rare. I'm not going to ask you if you understand. If you didn't you wouldn't be here. Undress."

She did, sensually but efficiently. The white cotton dress went first. Under was a pair of everyday panties, just white. No hose, only socks and shoes, as I had requested. Lingerie doesn't interest me. Bodies don't even interest me. She didn't interest me. But what I could do to her—that was what interested me.

She was naked. Her body was good. Not ideal, but with a warmth and reality to her. Big, full tits with just enough sag to mean reality and not silicone or somesuch. A plump little tummy. A plump mons with a gentle tuft of dark hair. It wasn't a body that you'd hang on your wall, but it was a body you'd want to fuck. But that was on her no list, which was fine by me. I definitely wanted to fuck with her, not just with her body.

Her hands kept drifting up, a force of will keeping them from hiding her breasts, covering her nipples. I smiled. SLUTSLAVE had a modest streak. Priceless.

I got out my toolbag, my own kind of wry smile on my face.

Other tops went on and on about their toys, pissing on each other about the quality of the leather, the weight, the evilness of certain objects. I sat back and watched them: wry grin then, wry grin now. If I had a headboard, I'd have it carved: *A workman is as good as his tools,* it would say. *A great one doesn't need them at all.*

I added it up once. Fifty dollars was as high as I got. Show me any other hobby that could give as much pleasure as my little bag of toys—or as much wonderful discomfort to SLUTSLAVE.

I laid them out on the rug in front of her. I felt like a surgeon—or a priest. "We're going to play a game," I said. "The rules are very simple. I ask a question. If you tell me the truth, you get a reward. If you don't, you get punished. Again, I won't ask if you understand."

I picked up a favorite—though, to tell my own truth, I like them all. This one was the favorite of the moment. I squeezed, and the clothespin yawned open. I held it out to her nipple, which, I noticed, was nicely wrinkled, and erect. "Are you wet?"

"Yes," she said in a breathy whisper. I could tell before she answered; her musk was thick in the room. I was hard. Hell, I was hard when I opened the front door, but hearing that, knowing that, my jeans grew that much tighter.

"First lesson. It's an important one. Sometimes even the truth can mean pain," I said, in my best of voices, as I released the spring on the clothespin, letting it bite down sharp and quick on her thickening nipple.

Her sigh was a lovely musical tone, a bass rumble of pain that peaked toward pleasure. Oh, yes, that was it. The first note of a long musical composition. Her knees buckled because of it, and I put a hand on her shoulder to steady her.

I kept it on for a mental beat of ten. Not long, but long enough. I released it, keeping my hand on her shoulder. It always hurts so much worse coming off than it does coming on. Sure enough, her knees buckled even more and she slipped, dropped down to my rug.

Still on her knees, breathing much more regularly, she looked up at me, chin level with my crotch. I knew if I said to, she'd unzip my fly, undo my belt, reach in with eager, strong fingers to fish out my dick, stick it into her hot mouth. She'd do it, I knew, but like the clothespin, it's so much better if you wait. So I did.

I stepped back, grinning at the flicker of disappointment on her face. You'll have to wait too, I thought. I retrieved my bag, and sat down in my chair, facing her. The clothespin was still in my hand and I found myself absently opening and closing it. A dom's worry bead, I guess. "Stand up. Right now."

She did. Her knees seemed a bit weak. "Come closer." She did, her gait slow and controlled. I reached down to my bag at my feet and picked up something new. "You're mine. You belong to me," I said, looking into her face. Her eyes shone. "I won't ask if you understand."

When I was a kid, I used to play with dolls. Well, maybe not "dolls," not exactly. No Raggedy Anns, no Barbies—not like that. I liked that they were mine, they belonged to me. I could make them do anything, at any time, and they didn't say a word. They just did it, forever smiling.

It was a new toy, another deceivingly simple thing. I saw it in some import/export place down in the city. Elegant and simple, black and glossy. Seeing it, I knew I had to have it. Having it, I couldn't wait to use it.

"Lean back," I said. I was tapping it against my palm, a lacquered metronome. Tilted back, her breasts swayed gently apart, only beginning to make that armpit migration—she was younger than I thought.

I ran the tip of the chopstick around her right nipple, feeling it skip and slide over her areola, the contours traveling down the length of it into my fingertips. She signed, softly.

Way back when, right after I outgrew those plastic dolls, I wondered if I had a dead thing—you know, preferring girls stiff and cold rather than warm and breathing. But that wasn't it. It wasn't their being immobile, plastic, it was my being in control, making them do what I wanted. Right then, she was my doll, my plaything, and I was completely in control.

I started tapping, steadily, almost softly at first. A smooth double-time. But after a dozen or so beats I moved it up to a harder, more insistent tempo. Her breathing quickened, started to grow close, to almost, maybe, match my beats with the lacquered stick. I watched her stomach rise and fall, a background accompaniment, echo to her hisses and signs.

I moved, circled her breast and nipple with my stick, painting her with the beats. *Tap, tap, tap, sigh, sigh, moan, sigh.* Then the other breast, but a little harder this time. She started to glow, shining with gentle sweat. I could smell her, a thick rutting musk. Now she really was wet.

Now only her nipples. Each impact steady, sure, quick, and hard. She started to unconsciously twist her body, a little this way, then the opposite, to get away from the beats. For a moment, I thought about stopping. Make her stand up, make her get dressed, kick her out for such a show of life and independence, but that would mean I'd have to stop using this lovely new toy. The stick as well as SLUTSLAVE.

Then I did stop. Time for the next movement. She lifted her head, looking long at me, breathing heavy and hard. Her eyes flicked with a bit of fear but more than anything, a kind of plea: *More.*

Back into the bag. Simple. When you have control, you don't

need gadgets, gizmos, fine leathers. Fifty dollars in the right
hands, with the right toy, and you have all you need. I came up
with a pair matching the first clip. Her eyes grew even wider, her
breathing deeper and quicker. She knew what was coming next.
I didn't have to say anything.

The right one first. I leaned down and held it there, open,
threatening around her so-hard nipple. She looked at it, then
looked at me. Again, fear, but more than anything a desire for
me to let go.

So I did. Her guttural bellow peaked threateningly toward a
scream but didn't as she swallowed and swallowed, hissed and
hissed it back down into herself. I was impressed.

I kept the clip on. It was wonderful to watch it bob up and
down with her steady, deep breaths. I could have watched it all
day, thinking: *This is mine. This is mine. This is mine.* I could
have, but I had another tit to play with.

Somewhere during all this, my cock had been confined,
trapped in my pants. Turning to the other tit, I felt how very,
very hard I'd gotten. But that would wait. I was in control here.
Not my dick.

The other one. Again, I held it there, looming over a tight
little point of nipple. Again, I let go.

This time a short, quick, honest scream blew past her lips.
Sound was a concern, but frankly, I didn't care. This was good—
damned good. She was a good toy, a good plaything. She was
mine to do with as I wanted.

I watched her, making sure the pain of the clips wasn't too
much for her. She whistled her breaths, in and out, belly rising and falling as she tried to accept, flow with, use, and enjoy
what was happening to her nipples, breasts, and body. I liked to
watch her, knowing that I was the cause of all this. Yes, my cock
was hard—steel, stone, rigid—in my pants, but this was almost

better. The bliss painting her body in shimmering sweat, making her pant and moan, making her clit twitch, wasn't something of mine that could ever go soft, ever come too quick. I could make her come and come and come again and never take off my pants.

Time for the next step. Both pins were in place, both nodded, dipped, and rose from their grips on her nipples as she squirmed against the pain. I picked up the chopstick again. "See this?" I said. She pulled herself up from her blurry rapture. Her eyes took a long time to focus. She looked, she nodded.

I tapped one clothespin, hard, sending serious shocks down through it into her already aching nipple. She squealed in shock, in endorphin delight. I did the same to the other, then back again. Back and forth. She was a wonderful plaything, a fun little toy. I enjoyed playing with her very much. Oh, the things we could do.

I glanced up at the clock. A qualifier of our time together rang in my mind. Just a few hours, she had said, to start. Time had flown.

"Listen to me," I said. Her vision was almost lost against the waves of sensation, but she managed to finally see me. "We're almost finished—for tonight, that is. But before we do, I'm going to fuck you."

She frowned past what was happening to her nipples, her tits, her body, her cunt. My words reached through it all and created a worry.

Not good to have my plaything in such a state. Time to demonstrate that I am in control, that for her, I'm the boss, I'm the Master—and she is merely a toy, and toys have nothing, not even a worry.

I reached into my bag at my feet, pulled it out, tossed it at her feet. "I said, I'm going to fuck you. My dick—right there in front of you—is going in your cunt. Do you have a problem with that?"

She didn't. The smell of her, the grin that flashed on her gleaming face, told me that. Her legs were already gently parted, the kind of reckless, unselfconscious display that only a plaything in the middle of a high-flying pleasure/pain/endorphin rush could have. She may have had a worry, but she was more a hungry cunt. A wet and ready cunt. A wet and very ready cunt with a rubber dick on the floor in front of her.

"Pick it up," I said, though I didn't have to, not really, "and fuck yourself with it."

She bent forward, picked it up. Parting her thighs a bit more, she showed me her pink wetness. The bare thatch of hair that descended from her mons was matted and gleaming with juice. Her lips were already gently apart, swollen and ready for my store-bought dick.

I knew I could probably have fucked her with my own cock, or simply unzipped my fly and stuck myself into her hot, wet mouth. But that would mean I was flesh and blood, a man, and not the Master I really was. A Master is cold, a Master knows what to do with a plaything, a toy, a doll. I knew what to do. That's what I lived for: that dominance, that authority, that control.

She slipped the dildo into herself, just an inch to start. Then out, then in deeper, with a slow twist. She bit her lip in concentration, she closed her eyes in bliss—lost to the pain in her tits, the cock in her cunt.

Kneeling on my rug, legs very wide, she fucked herself. The gentle part ended quickly. She was now really, strongly fucking herself. A soft foam rimmed her cunt where the plastic slicked in and out. Some of her pubic hairs streaked along the length on the outstroke, curled in on the return. The hiss that had been only from the clips on her nipples was joined by the deeper sounds of a rolling, approaching come.

I didn't know her that well, but a good Master knows the sounds, no matter the toy, and I could tell that she could see it coming, could smell, taste it coming. Her breathing broke, became shorter, panting. *Now, right now,* I thought as I bent forward and put thumbs and fingers on the pins. I pulled.

Her eyes snapped open, fear lighting her irises. This time she didn't say, without words, *more,* but rather *Oh my God.*

I pulled. Not hard, just enough to drag her orgasm out, draw it farther out. Her fucking had slowed, eased, but she was too far along to stop. She couldn't if she wanted to.

I didn't want her to. So she didn't. I didn't need to say it, she understood it: the language of Master to SLUTSLAVE. Her fucking increased, pushing herself back up to the precipice. It didn't take long for her to be looking down the fast slope to her come. This time she said, without words, *now.*

Yes, SLUTSLAVE: *Now.* The pins came off. Screw noise concerns. Her scream came from her nipples, her tits, but also from her spasming, quivering, quaking cunt. Her come rattled her, making her body shake and her head bob back and forth. Her legs, already tensed from holding her forward, collapsed, spilling her backward on my old scratchy rug.

I watched her. Her breathing, after a long while, eased to a regular, resting rhythm. Then I went to my bathroom, got a big fluffy towel, and draped it over her. She didn't say anything, not even thanks.

I got her a glass of water from my kitchen, even put a little slice of lemon in it. She took it with gently quivering fingers. Drank all of it, handed it back. Then she said, "Thanks," but for the glass or the evening I didn't know.

Slowly, she got up, started hunting for her panties. I helped her, handing them over to her. She seemed to be happy.

Finally, she was dressed, though she looked funny with her hair messed. "Are you okay to go home?" I asked her, my hand on her arm. "Should I call you a cab?"

"I'm—whooo," she breathed, laughing for a second with a shivering after-feeling. "I'm okay. Really. Thank you," she finally said. "That was a blast."

"I'm glad. I'd love to do it again some time—soon."

"So would I. Really." Her hand was on the doorknob.

"Write me," I said, holding it open for her. "Send me a message and we'll pick a date."

"That'd be fun. Sure." She walked down the hall. When she got to the end she turned, waved to me. I waved back.

I checked my messages an hour or so later. Nothing. I watched some television, something I barely remember. Cops, I think. Or doctors. Something like that. Before I went to bed, I checked again. Nothing. I sent her a message: "Hope you had a good time. Write when you get a chance."

In the morning, nothing. I browsed some of the chatrooms, even though I'd never known her to be there that early. Nothing, of course.

When I got home from work I checked again. Spam. A few messages from some friends. Nothing. She's just busy. Things happen, I told myself, not believing my own thoughts.

Before I went to bed I wrote another message. But I didn't send it. Maybe in a few days, I thought.

I checked again the instant I walked in after work. Nothing. Nothing at all. I wrote her, against my better judgment. Simple, direct: "Concerned about how you're feeling. Please write."

That will do it, I thought. That'll reach her. Was it too much to ask? I thought she had fun. I thought she did.

But when I went to bed there was nothing but more spam, a few other messages. Nothing from her.

Around midnight, late for me, I went to bed. Nothing at all. I tried to masturbate but it didn't work out.

Eventually I fell asleep.

In the morning I checked again, first thing. Nothing. Nothing at all.

I never used the handle MASTER017 again.

A GOOD REFERENCE

Mackenzie Cross

"To train is to be taught."
– From the unpublished notebooks
of Alexander Waring.

"But what's in it for me?" the voice whined.

It was becoming increasingly difficult to maintain an attitude of professional calm. A trainer must cultivate patience, I reminded myself carefully. But even Master Chou himself might have had his balance challenged by Ms. Elizabeth Harding. She had repeated this question for the third time in the space of fifteen minutes.

I took a few moments to collect myself by pretending to examine her dossier again. I had it all memorized before our interview, which hadn't proven difficult. It contained a single sheet of paper and a photograph. The attractive, blonde woman in the photo was wearing black heels, a leather corset, and not much else. The all-too-predictable spread-leg pose left no doubt that her conformist cunt was, unsurprisingly, hairless.

Contrary to the time-honored rule, this gentleman does not prefer blondes and she was no exception. I do not care for a completely shaved pussy either. I consider it an indication of laziness in a submissive.

The application form gave the matching details. Ms. Elizabeth Harding from Toronto, Canada, was twenty-six years old, stood halfway between five and six feet tall, weighed one hundred and fifteen pounds, and had measurements of 35/23/37 with a C cup size. She had no known medical conditions. She had never been spanked, never been whipped, and never been bound. She had never even heard of BDSM. When asked why she was here, she replied it was a birthday present from her boyfriend, Henry.

To call Elizabeth Harding a virgin newbie would have been to grant her a title far in excess of her station. I glanced at the photo again. Was that really a studded leather collar she was wearing? It was difficult to hold back a sigh of exasperation.

I hated working with newbies then, and I still hate working with them. They're more trouble than they're worth: either convinced of their own intrinsic value, or clueless that they might have any value at all. But at the time Elizabeth Harding walked into my office, I needed the money. It was still early in my career and it had been some time since my last assignment. I could not afford the luxury of turning down jobs, even though I was sorely tempted in this case.

I impressed myself with how perfectly normal my voice sounded. "As I explained, Ms. Harding, I train submissives. Many women find a great deal of satisfaction and fulfillment in fully exploring this aspect of their character. Relationships are often enhanced when a woman becomes more accepting of her submissive nature, and frequently the quality of the sexual experience can be dramatically improved."

"But ... I would have to do everything you told me, right?"

"Yes, that is one of the conditions."

"Even if you told me to clean your house?"

"Yes, that is a possibility."

"And you can even tell me not to come?" There was that whine again. It tickled my brain with the delicate subtlety of a chainsaw. I closed my eyes and sought my balance. I could see where this was going.

"Yes, Ms. Harding, I would control everything, even your orgasms. That is part of the contract that exists between the trainer and the submissive." There, didn't that make perfect sense? What could have possibly been clearer?

"Well, that sounds pretty good for you, Mr. Waring, but what's in it for me?"

There have only been a few times in my life that I have deliberately considered doing bodily harm to another human being. This was one of them. If I hadn't needed to pay the rent, I would've thrown the bitch out right then and there and gone back to my writing. This interview was not going well.

Master Chou had warned me that situations such as these were inevitable. I could almost hear his words, a dry, dusty whispering of sound: "When all seems *yang*, Alexander, that is when you must look for *yin*. Search it out."

And then, in a moment I would later realize as a true epiphany, a turning point in my career, my gaze fastened on the credenza beside my desk. There sat the little Buddha figurine that was Krista's graduation gift to me, to thank me for her training. Carved from an exceptional piece of rich imperial emerald jade, the smiling Buddha looked happy and content.

I felt a weight lift from my shoulders. Balance returned in that instant, and with it, the solution to my problem. I allowed myself the luxury of a moment's reflection. Elizabeth Harding would wait on my pleasure a while.

Krista was my fourth assignment and had proven a most interesting challenge. She was a mature female who had chosen to explore her slavish nature in the middle years of her life. Setting aside her fears, she contacted me and asked to be trained. She had not required much in the way of technical training; she was well read and understood the mechanics of service. Rather, the challenges had been both practical and emotional.

We lived over a thousand miles apart. Because physical contact was limited, much of the work had to be done by telephone. During the months of her training, there were less than a half dozen actual sessions.

Of greater import was her ability to trust. Whilst she would readily give up her body for abuse—she was a pain slut of the first order—her mind was closed behind walls and fortifications of fear and doubt. She did not yield her surrender easily. I invented new training techniques just for her case.

The disciplines and regimes had proven successful and we were both pleased with the results. Krista finally experienced the complete joy of submission to another. While still unowned, she was greatly more content. She knew herself to be capable of offering herself fully, and had a benchmark to use for evaluating potential dominants. We've kept in contact since the end of her training.

More importantly, some of the techniques I developed for Krista would help resolve my current problem.

Across the desk, Ms. Harding had begun to fidget, still waiting for my reply. I glanced at my watch. It was just shy of three in the afternoon. Krista would be home and by herself. Perfect.

"Would you excuse me for a moment, Ms. Harding? There is a telephone call I must make. It won't take long. Thank you."
I didn't give her a chance to respond, but lifted the receiver and dialed Krista's number from memory.

The phone rang a few times before Krista answered. "Hello?" Even when her submission was not completely upon her, there was still a lovely, sultry quality to her voice—a contralto pitch with a hint of gravel, Billie Holiday on a good day.

"Hello, Krista."

There was the briefest of pauses at the other end of the line. I knew the subtle transformations now taking place. Breathing would deepen as she sharpened her focus. Pulse would increase and her body temperature would elevate slightly. There would be changes to her body posture as well; her back would straighten, legs open, and she would position her right hand in a familiar way. Her cunt would begin to juice and throb. Krista always responded well to control.

"Hello, Sir. This one is joyful to hear her trainer's voice again. How may Krista serve?" Her voice was now just above a whisper, soft and breathy, with a tremolo of arousal. Voice training was an area of particular emphasis in Krista's development. I found myself growing hard listening to her response.

Third-person speech had been a particular challenge for Krista. She struggled hard and had been punished more than once for failures with this discipline. Now it was her preferred mode of speaking to dominants.

"Krista, attend my words. I am in my office interviewing a girl who may wish to be trained. She is unsure of the potential benefits, and I intend to use you as a demonstration of what may be achieved. Acknowledge."

"Yes, Sir. Krista understands."

"Go to the bedroom, girl. Disrobe and lie down on the bed. Acknowledge when this has been done."

I glanced up at Ms. Harding. Her eyes had gone wide. She was probably unaware of her dropped jaw and open mouth. This was going to be a new experience for her. I pressed the speaker button on the phone and replaced the handset on the cradle.

"You ask an excellent question, Elizabeth, and although I have tried to answer you, I have obviously been unsuccessful up to now." I was using my trainer's voice now: confident, assured, with an element of menace, a lion stalking prey. "However, I propose a demonstration. If, at its conclusion, you still do not wish to avail yourself of my services, I will gladly refund your deposit."

"What demonstration?" The whine was gone. She was in unfamiliar territory.

"Sit quietly and you will understand shortly." The words were said in the way a trainer might speak to a submissive.

From the speaker came the sounds of zippers and Velcro, then the springs of a bed being weighted.

"Krista is ready, Sir."

My eyes were fixed on Elizabeth, drawing her into the experience, forcing her to become part of the ménage. "Release, Krista. You have sixty seconds. You may use your hands."

"Yes, Sir. This one obeys." I pointed to the clock on the desk. Ms. Harding took a quick glance at the clock, then returned to be held by my gaze. Thirty seconds later came the sounds of female orgasm, a sharp staccato of screams, punctuated with gasps for air. The release took an additional thirty seconds. Ms. Harding was blushing, but could not look away.

"Thank you, Sir. Thank you." The words were said on the heels of the last gasps, colouring them with the essence of erotic rapture.

"Again, Krista," my voice was cold, deep, demanding.

"Yes, Sir." This time she needed only forty-five seconds, but her screams were even more desperate.

"Oh, God! Thank you, Sir. Thank you, thank you." Krista always came well, but I could tell that she was especially enjoying this experience. Not only was she releasing for me and gaining satisfaction from performing a service for her trainer, but she also loved to expose herself to others. All this combined to make her releases intense and noisy.

Elizabeth Harding's blush had deepened. I noted with interest the way her hands tightly gripped the arms of the chair and the unconscious spreading of her legs.

Her eyes were still held captive by my gaze, unable to tear herself away. Perhaps she had some potential, after all.

I allowed Krista a moment of rest. "Of course, Elizabeth, any female can be trained to orgasm on command without too much difficulty. But my training goes somewhat beyond these ordinary techniques." I paused for a moment and tilted my head slightly toward the speakerphone. "Krista, attend my words. Take your dildo, the large one, and fuck yourself. You will beg for permission to come."

"Y ... yes, Sir," she said, with a trace of fear in her voice. Krista knew that permission was not always granted.

There was the sound of a night table drawer being opened. My cool gaze never left Elizabeth's eyes as Krista's screams began. I felt the familiar sense of power as my control was extended to these two highly dissimilar women. I still did not care for the blonde newbie, but the exercise of control is always a pleasure to a dominant.

It didn't take long before Krista began to beg, "Please, Sir? This girl is ready ... this girl needs to release." The words were said as she exhaled, breathy and needful.

"Permission denied, Krista. Continue. Harder." My voice was deep and cold, a frozen barrier of domination that she would not dare to cross. On the other side of the table, Elizabeth began to squirm in her seat. Her breathing was becoming rapid, deepening her flush.

The only sounds in the room were moans and grunts as I proxy fucked Krista. They were animal sounds, the rutting of a beast.

"Sir! Please now, Sir? Let Krista come, please ... Sir? Sir!!!" Krista's voice was a frantic plea. It filled my office with submissive desperation.

"No."

"Let her come, Mr. Waring! She really needs to." Elizabeth's voice held only a mild echo of the drama in Krista's words, but I was pleased to note a sense of sisterhood in her statement. The whine was gone, replaced with the husky sweetness of a female in heat. She felt Krista's need. It was a beginning. I shook my head slightly in negation.

"Why not? Why are you being so cruel? What kind of bastard are you?" But her heart really wasn't in her words. She was too caught up in the moment.

Meanwhile Krista's sounds had grown to a frenzy of lust. "Oh, God, Sir! Krista begs. Krista begs! Please, please ... Sir? Oh fuck ... Sir? She can't hold it, Sir! She can't ... It's too big. Krista pleads! Sir!!"

"No, Krista."

"Aiiee!!!" But she didn't stop fucking herself. Krista had been well trained. Elizabeth, on the other hand, had not ... yet.

"Please, Mr. Waring. Please tell her to come. I hate to hear her in such agony."

" 'Please'? What an interesting choice of words, Elizabeth." I raised one eyebrow as I considered her request, keeping my voice calm and conversational. "You asked what was in it for you. Observe, girl, while I demonstrate."

I changed the pitch of my voice louder so that Krista would hear over her primal screams. "Now, Krista. Release for your trainer."

Krista's orgasm lasted for over two minutes. Lovely, undulating gasps and screams as the pulsing waves of her release racked her body. Throughout it all, I observed Elizabeth. Her body shuddered in sympathetic vibration with Krista, her thighs pressed tightly together. At one point her eyes closed, deeply involving herself in the experience.

"Oh, God!! Thank you, Sir. Oh, thank you. This slut thanks her trainer ..." I hung up on Krista in the middle of her thanks. She had satisfied my purpose.

I continued to stare at Ms. Elizabeth Harding.

"You could do that for me? Make me come that way? Really?"

"There is that possibility, Elizabeth. There is no guarantee, but it is possible."

She took a deep breath as she made up her mind. "Okay, I'll do it. When do we start?"

My voice changed to training mode. "Right now, girl. We shall begin with basic postures. Come here so I may instruct you how to kneel. After that ..."

Elizabeth's training had begun. She was no Krista, but I was not displeased with the results.

And what did I learn? What was my epiphany? A simple truth: There is nothing like a good reference to help you sell your product, eh?

Thank you, Krista.

BOARDROOM ETIQUETTE

Lee Ash

"Is this likely to go on much longer?"

Rather than staring at Kirsty Summers, who was the acting head of the finance department and chairperson for that afternoon's meeting, Carter studied his Rolex. His expression was weary. His Filofax was open on the boardroom table before him. He held his cell phone, ready to make calls, shuffle appointments, and renegotiate the remainder of his day's schedule.

His question brought a stunned silence to the room.

The somber-suited executives around him drew startled gasps. From the periphery of his vision he saw those sitting closest shift position in their seats as though they were trying to put distance between him and themselves.

Kirsty Summers turned the full force of her legendary sarcasm on him.

She was a pretty woman, petite and smartly dressed in her plain black jacket and matching skirt, and she was known in the office for being a high achiever. But she had a reputation for stamping on the fingers of those climbing the lower rungs of the corporate ladder. And that reputation came with the disclaimer that she was a merciless bitch.

Kirsty waited until the silence was at its most painful before she spoke. "Is this likely to go on much longer?" she repeated. "I'm sorry, Mr. Carter. Do you have a date?"

Someone snickered.

Seemingly encouraged by the laughter, Kirsty continued to glower at him. "I truly am sorry, Mr. Carter. I had no idea that my finance management meeting intruded on your valuable time."

"'Intruded' isn't the word I would have used," Carter said coolly. He glanced up from his Filofax and flexed a charming smile. "I think 'encroached' would be a more appropriate term."

Her cheeks turned pink.

She opened her mouth to speak but he chose that moment to continue. It was an old trick, designed to make the interrupted person look as though they didn't know how to conduct a civilized conversation. "I came here to contribute to a finance management meeting that was scheduled from two until three." Pointedly checking his watch again, Carter said, "It's now quarter past three."

"I can tell the time."

"You've had an hour and fifteen minutes of my undivided attention." He carried on as though she hadn't spoken. "And I imagine my three o'clock appointment is currently experiencing the same level of animosity that's apparent on your face."

Kirsty blushed as though she had been trying to keep her anger secret.

It had been easy to get her flustered, and Carter marveled that he had never thought to try this tactic before. His grin inched wider. "If necessity forces me to overrun on each of my remaining appointments, I'll waste the remainder of the day apologizing to every subsequent client."

"And that would be my fault?" Kirsty sneered.

"It's good of you to acknowledge the fact," Carter said calmly. His smile glinted brighter in the brief flash of her anger. "But I'm not looking to apportion blame at the moment. I'm just trying to find out how much longer this interminable meeting will continue."

She had been using a wooden ruler to point to the various slices of the pie chart from her PowerPoint projection. She slammed it hard and swift against the boardroom table. The retort was like a gunshot. "Cancel your three o'clock, Mr. Carter." She swept her glare around the other executives. Bright spots of color rouged her cheeks. "The meeting is over now. We'll reconvene same time next week and pick up where we left off. If you can all clear the room as quickly as possible, I think Mr. Carter and I should use the remaining time alone to discuss boardroom etiquette."

Carter had his cell phone pressed to his ear and held up a finger to silence Kirsty. Without acknowledging her, he directed his full attention to the telephone call. "I'm sorry to do this to you, Guy," he began. "You've probably guessed I can't make our three o'clock."

He paused and listened.

"No, it wasn't deliberate. Just a boring finance meeting that overran."

From the corner of his eye he could see Kirsty's eyes widen with outrage. A passing executive flinched as though stung by shrapnel.

"Yes," Carter continued. "It was her." There was another pause and then he chuckled into the phone. "That would be one way to keep her quiet," he agreed. "Call me tomorrow lunchtime and we'll reschedule." He glanced up to meet the thunderous fury on Kirsty's face. Smiling blithely, he snapped the phone shut and said, "I've cancelled my three o'clock. I'm all yours now. Let's have our discussion on boardroom etiquette."

The other executives fled. Sensing the horror of an impending eruption, and clearly aware that such disasters could inflict collateral damage on innocent bystanders, they snatched their bags, cases, and notepads and hurried from the boardroom. Carter had thought a couple of them might linger out of ghoulish curiosity. Clashes at the executive level were grist for the rumor mill of the office gossips. Firsthand accounts invariably lifted the reporter to the highest status amongst the rubberneck brigade. But it seemed that no one from the finance meeting had the balls to witness this battle from the immediate sidelines. Either that or, more likely, Carter thought, they were so weary from an hour and a quarter of Kirsty's banal chatter on the subject of finance management that they were thankful for any excuse to hurry from the room.

When the door slammed closed he was alone with Kirsty Summers.

She fixed him with a glare that would have scared a lesser man.

"Before I submit my official complaint to the CEO," Kirsty growled, "would you like to tell me what the hell you thought you were doing just then?"

"I was publicly humiliating you," he replied. He rested back in his seat and asked, "Did it work?"

Her jaw dropped.

"You look angry and embarrassed," he grinned. Lazily, he climbed from his seat. "I can imagine that the other members of the finance management meeting are busy discussing you, even as we speak. Does that make you feel ashamed? Does that get you sopping at the gusset?"

"You bastard," she exclaimed.

"Does it make your snatch hot? Is your crotch dripping right now as you ponder the embarrassment of being talked about by all those executives who think they're so much better than you? All those men who keep saying you're a woman and not able to do this job?"

"You lousy, fucking bastard!"

Without warning she hurled herself at him.

The tussle was over before it began.

Carter had expected the attack and caught her wrists before her nails could rake him. He turned her around, pushed her facedown over the boardroom table, and stopped her struggles by pressing his body on top of hers. A fug of cloying sweat rose from her body. She wriggled and writhed to escape him, striking at the table and lashing out with her arms and legs. Carter pressed himself more firmly against her until, after a moment, she fell still.

"Didn't I promise you a thrill at this meeting?" Carter whispered.

She moaned. It was a sound that could have been borne out of anger, frustration, or satisfaction.

"Last night, when you begged me to spank you, and then pleaded for me to fuck you up the ass, didn't I promise you the thrill of a lifetime?"

Kirsty panted heavily beneath him. Aside from the heated sweat that rose from her body, he could also sense the sweet fragrance of her sex. The scent was strong enough to make his erection throb with renewed anticipation. Moving her wrists so that he held them both in one large hand, Carter shifted his free fingers to her legs. Sliding his touch beneath the hem of her short skirt, inching his fingers higher over the bare flesh of her inner thighs, he finally reached the broiling warmth of her crotch. A thin shield of cotton protected the lips of her pussy but the fabric was dewy with wetness. Her heat was so powerful it was like dipping his fingers into molten wax. Firmly, he pushed two fingers against the sopping gusset.

Kirsty whimpered.

"I was right, wasn't I?" he chuckled. "You are enjoying the thrill of a lifetime, aren't you?"

He knew to tense himself for her response. He was goading her and it was Kirsty's nature to battle against every insult or provocation, regardless of how much she desired such base treatment. She cursed with vitriolic fluency and threw her body into bucking spasms as she tried to pull away from him.

Carter pushed his fingers deeper.

He entered her with his fingers sheathed by her panties. Ordinarily he knew the penetration might have been uncomfortable. But experience had taught him that this level of humiliation invariably fueled Kirsty's strongest arousal. She was warm and wet around his hand. His fingers and the cotton slid easily into her confines. Every eager breath she snatched assured him that she was appreciating his domination.

"Do you know what Guy said you needed?" Carter breathed.

She grunted.

He could tell her anger was at the same level as her desire for him. She was a beautiful woman and he adored her with genuine affection. But her submissive nature was offset by an assertive personality. The control she yearned for had to be administered with a ruthless hand. His erection throbbed harder when he realized that he was the man she had chosen to deliver that control.

"Guy said you needed a cock in your mouth to shut you up."

"I'll have him fired."

"You'll do no such thing," Carter snapped. He snatched his hand from between her legs, grimacing at having to give up his contact with the warm haven of her cleft. Hearing her groan with equal dismay only provided a small satisfaction. Determined to enforce his authority on her, Carter grabbed a fistful of hair and dragged her away from the table. She fell to her knees in front of his crotch. Her open mouth was on the same level as the bulge in his pants. "You won't have Guy fired. You'll prove him right. And you'll suck me off now."

Slowly, he peeled his zipper downward.

If there had ever been any worry that Kirsty didn't want this, that doubt evaporated when he watched her hungrily lick her lips. Her eyes glinted and opened wide at the sight of his exposed erection. Her smile turned greedy. Without hesitation, she stroked her tongue along his length.

The sensation was an exquisite caress. The warm, fluid sensation of her tongue against his shaft was enough to push him to the point of climax. Carter stiffened as he tried to stop himself from coming too soon in this game.

He pulled tight on her hair.

"Don't lick it," he grunted. "I didn't ask you to lick it. I want this stuffed in your mouth, keeping you silent."

She glared up at him. Her expression was etched with a furious resentment. But her eyes shone with a bright need that mirrored his own.

This was what he liked best about Kirsty. It was always a challenge to know whether he had pushed her far enough and to make sure she was enjoying what they did. Her prudish exterior was a heavily reinforced façade. She presented herself as a prim and proper executive, a dictionary definition of the word *respectable*. But her true nature was far less puritanical.

His erection disappeared into her mouth.

She suckled greedily against him, making the animal sounds of a sow at a trough. Her austere composure was gone as her flushed cheeks bulged and she threw herself into the task of fitting his entire cock in her mouth.

Carter's dick brushed over her tongue and then pressed at the back of her throat. She sucked on him without finesse or grace. It was obvious she was driven by an avaricious thirst. It had taken an effort to restrain his climax when she licked at him before. Now it took a magnificent display of control to stave off his eruption.

"Guy was right," he grunted. "I must tell him."

She pulled her face away. His cock hung between them, the shaft glistening with her saliva. A lengthening string of pre-come stretched from his glans to her lower lip.

"You won't tell him any such thing," she hissed.

Carter frowned.

"Can you see how right Guy was?" he muttered. "As soon as my cock's out of your mouth, you start talking again." Tugging her hair, forcing her face back toward his shaft, he urged her to suck on him again.

Her gaze flashed with brief resentment. She resisted the pull of his hand at her scalp for a moment. And then she began to devour him with fresh enthusiasm. Her fingers went to his thighs. She gripped him so tight her nails pressed through the linen of his pants and into his flesh. And all the time she seemed desperate to fit more of his dick into her mouth.

Carter closed his eyes and wondered if she deserved punishing before they concluded this lesson on boardroom etiquette. The wooden ruler Kirsty had used remained on the table. He toyed briefly with the idea of using it to stripe her backside. The idea was extremely tempting, and he could almost picture her pale buttocks slashed with crimson lines. In his mind's eye he could hear her containing her cries, stiffening beneath each blow of the ruler, and struggling not to be influenced by the pleasure of the pain. He pushed the thoughts away, sure they would drive him beyond the limits of his own control.

She slurped noisily around him. One hand still clutched his leg. The other had disappeared between her thighs. Above the sounds of her wetly munching at his erection he could hear the fluid slurp of her fingers sliding in and out of her sex. He hadn't given her permission to touch herself but, with his arousal this strong, he didn't think such an exercise in control would be productive. He glanced down and saw that the hem of her skirt had risen high enough to expose the tops of her thighs. She hadn't bothered to remove her panties and, just as he had penetrated her before, Kirsty rubbed herself through the flimsy fabric.

He could make out the distinct shape of her labia fluidly molded against the cotton. Her fingers worked faster and her sighs grew louder and less articulate. With his fingers wound tight in her hair he could feel the first tremors of satisfaction as they built inside her. When her orgasm came—surprisingly muted but obvious in its own subtle way—he watched eddies of satisfaction ripple easily through her body.

She continued to suck as the pleasure ran its course. Her eyes were closed, joyous tears trailing down her cheeks as she basked in the experience.

Carter guessed she was trying to keep her release and satisfaction secret from him. But he caught the full fragrance of her climax as it burst from her loins and spurted wetly into the crotch of her panties. Because he was used to seeing the pink flush that colored her cheeks and because he knew her so well that he could recognize the delectable scent of her climax, Carter wasn't fooled by her pretense.

He allowed himself to come.

Relaxing his efforts for a moment, allowing the orgasm to shoot along the length of his cock and fill her mouth, he kept his hand fixed tightly at the back of her head as his shaft repeatedly pulsed against her throat. Slowly, he released his hold on Kirsty's hair and pushed her away.

"That was okay," he muttered.

She glared at him and wiped a smear of semen from her lower lip. Her throat continued to work as she struggled to swallow. He saw a film of his ejaculate coat her tongue when she opened her mouth to feign dismay.

"That was it?" she asked bitterly.

She had already made the transformation from submissive to superior. Even though she was still on her knees—her cheeks flushed from pleasure and the crotch of her panties sopping—she assumed the role with an ease that was almost admirable. "You promised me the thrill of a lifetime," she reminded him. "Are you saying that was it? Does this end now, with you spent and me swallowing the taste of your come?"

Her words were ragged with breathlessness. Carter could see she was still trembling and he guessed her orgasm had been a powerful one, regardless of the fact that she'd kept it subdued. But he could see no point in arguing about whether or not she had been satisfied.

Kirsty snorted with contempt and asked, "Is that your idea of giving a girl the thrill of a lifetime?"

Carter laughed and shook his head. He pushed his flaccid cock back in his pants and began to tidy up his Filofax and papers from the table. "That wasn't the thrill of a lifetime I'd promised," he admitted. "That was just a taster. The real thrill comes next week."

She regarded him warily.

"Unless you apologize to me in front of all the executives," he continued, "we'll have another of these meetings on board-room etiquette."

"And that's going to be as big a thrill as this was?" she asked scornfully.

He nodded. "It should be. Next week I'll insist on having a third party attend while we discuss boardroom etiquette." He paused for a moment to reflect on his words and added, "I think Guy might be available."

Her eyes opened wide and she stared at him with features torn between horror and enthusiasm. Carter didn't know whether or not she would make the apology at the next meeting. And he hadn't completely decided whether or not he wanted to share Kirsty with anyone else from the office. But, as long as she thought there was a danger of that happening, Carter knew she would spend the rest of the week anticipating the humiliation. Because he knew her drives and desires, he figured that expectation would be enough to give Kirsty the thrill of a lifetime.

THE SUN IS AN ORDINARY STAR

Shanna Germain

He was cleaning the bedroom for Stella's return when he heard it. He'd been down on his haunches, swishing the broom beneath the bed's dark corners, when something metallic clanked against the broom. He fished it out.

There, among the dust bunnies and dirt, was Stella's favorite set of nipple clamps, two silver clips connected by a thin chain. The metal was dusty and a few of Stella's long hairs were wound in the chain. Still on his haunches, he picked the clamps up. They were lighter than he remembered, more fragile, the weight of them in his palm almost nothing.

He opened one of the large clips, ran his finger across the row of teeth. Croc heads, Stella called them. Before everything, she'd call home from the office some days, leave a message on the machine. "You're going to have to get out the crocs tonight," she'd say.

Last time she'd called home was right before Christmas. She'd been working on the big holiday shoe campaign, Photoshopping sweat and muscles and boobs onto famous athletes. Even on the message her voice was shaky. "Baby, I'm not feeling up to par," she said. "Let's get those alligator maws out tonight. And whatever else you can think of. I know you're gonna make me feel better."

And he had. As soon as she'd walked in the door, still in her cream-colored work pants and the brown blouse that matched her eyes, her long dark hair pulled back, he'd ordered her to undress. She looked tired, light gray circles under her big brown eyes, but she'd asked and he always tried to give her what she asked for. He'd ordered her to undress him, too, and then he'd cuffed her arms to their slatted headboard. She was pale curves against the purple bedspread. Her long hair, loose from its clip, waved out around her head.

With her arms above her head, her small tits tilted upward. He loved her tits, pale and down-fuzzed as summer peaches, but it was her nipples that he loved the most, the way they stretched high and taut when she was aroused. He'd teased her first, rubbing the sharp edge of the clamp teeth along the inside of her thigh, around the edges of her neck, in smaller and smaller circles around her nipples. He loved to watch the points push into her skin.

Stella was as still as he'd told her to be, mouth closed, only her flared nostrils giving away her arousal. When he saw she was wet, he slid the opened clamp along the edge of her pussy lips, up to her clit. He'd never clamped her there, but he'd promised her it was coming. Now he closed the clamp, just a bit, on that pale pink flesh. She arched her back and gasped.

He took the clamps away, slapped the curvy bottom of her ass, hard enough to feel the sting on his palm. "Be still," he said.

She closed her eyes, her nostrils flaring. When her eyes were closed, he opened both clamps and then closed them on the rosy skin of her nipples. Stella inhaled deeply through her nose.

He leaned back and watched her, the metal clips closed onto her taut flesh, leaving little pinpoints of bloodless skin. At the end of the bed, Stella's feet, the only thing she couldn't keep still, arched in their bonds. Her clit was aching, he knew. "You want to be fucked?" he asked.

Stella knew enough to keep quiet, even to shake her head a little from side to side.

He put one finger inside the hot wetness of her, curled it into an arch. "No?" he asked.

"No," she said. But her pussy gave her away, the way she stretched against her bonds to take more of his finger inside her. He entered her with a second finger.

"You're sure?" he asked. He loved to watch her at this moment. His Stella, stubborn as her Aries sign, truth-speaking, Type A. The internal struggle—to say what she wanted, to take what she wanted, or to give up to him, just for these few moments. This, he knew, was why she wanted to be topped, needed to be topped. This was why he loved it. His cock loved it too, of course, but his mind loved to get her here, to this final release.

He wriggled his fingers inside her, hard against her walls. "I'm sorry, what?" he said, even though she hadn't said anything.

"No," she breathed. Just once. But he knew it was enough. He took his fingers out. "Look at me," he said. And she did, while he entered her, his cock going deep inside her and one hand pulling the nipple clamps, hard and harder, until she begged to be let loose.

He reached up and unbuckled the cuffs. "One hand on your clit." She did as he said, she put one hand on her clit, two fingers rubbing furiously back and forth. The sight of her was almost enough to make him come.

He entered her again, keeping himself back far enough that she could still work her clit. Her other hand reached for something to hold on to. "The clamps," he said. "Pull."

And she did, pulling her nipples up and up with the chain, arching her back to press her clit into him and her hand. He came before she did, but was hard enough to keep inside until she came. Her orgasm was soft, quiet moans and one last tug on the clamps.

He eased himself out of her, and sat beside her on the bed. When he took the clamps from her nipples, she moaned again, turning her head away. He kissed her nipples gently. She turned back toward him, her brown eyes no longer squinted-up from stress. She still looked tired though, beneath her eyes and around the edges of her lips. He stroked her hair and she snuggled her face into the curve of his neck. "You always know exactly what I need," she said. And then she'd fallen asleep, her breath soft and quiet against his skin.

That was six weeks, two surgeries, and some kind of newfangled chemo ago. Today, Stella was coming home. He didn't know what to do with the clamps, and he couldn't bear to touch the cold metal any longer, so he opened the nightstand drawer.

The books from friends and family—*Coping with Cancer, Outsmart Your Cancer, Cancer Husband*—stared up at him, spines uncracked. He'd tried to read the *Husband* one during one of Stella's appointments, but he hadn't understood what was about to happen, and the chapters on lumpectomy and chemo and sex with cancer had seemed impossible. Now, he wished he'd read it, at least the sex chapter, although he doubted there was anything about the kind of sex he and Stella had. *Used* to have. They'd had sex once or twice while she was sick, but it had been the kind of soft, gentle sex he'd always imagined belonged to virgins and old people. When Stella's bones hurt after hot showers and she couldn't sleep because the sheets tore at her skin, they'd fallen into this habit of moving quietly together, him raising himself above her, cock and pussy the only place they touched. And then even that had fallen away, forgotten under the bed in the midst of doctors and options and books and Stella's determination.

Stella had tackled cancer the same way she tackled a big project at work, or, when he'd first met her, a research paper in grad school. Learn the facts, make a to-do list, and then checkmark your way down to the end. Get diagnosed, check. Find the best doctor they could afford, check. Explore all the treatments, check. Get rid of it, check. He didn't want to admit it, but Stella had handled all this with her usual grace and determination, while he was the one who felt lost.

Now, they had cut it out of her body, and she was coming home to him. And he felt like the world's biggest asshole for what he wanted. Or the world's whiniest husband: *My wife went to Cancerville and all I got was this stupid T-shirt.* He wanted her down on her knees, the gorgeous globes of her ass pink-marked, begging him for mercy. He wanted to tie her up and enter her, one half-inch at a time, until she bucked her hips against him. He wanted to clamp the clips in his hand around the points of her nipples and force her to fuck herself until she came, until the tightness left her body and she could fall asleep again, at the point of his neck, without worry. He wanted to give her that release, but without topping her, without hurting a body that had already been beaten by its own cells, but he didn't know how.

Simply the possibility of it made his cock harden. He reached down to rub himself through his pants, and then he realized he was still holding the nipple clamps. Shiny guilt-makers. He dropped them onto the pile of books and shut the drawer tight. It was almost time to pick Stella up anyway.

Stella came home from the hospital with a new pair of reading glasses and a new star, dark red against her pale skin. He saw the glasses as soon as she got in the car—she put the blue- and yellow-striped frames on so she could see the street signs, even though she wasn't driving. He hadn't seen the star yet, but he felt it radiating from her body, sending heat through her white T-shirt, through the blue fleece she wore over it, through the shawl she had wrapped around her shoulders. The heat made him feel like he'd landed on the surface of some unknown sun. Sweat started at the edges of his hairline.

In the seat beside him, Stella shivered. He took his hand off the window button.

"Temperature okay?" he asked. She turned from the window. Her now-short hair was peppered with early gray above her ears. The pinkish tint of the glasses turned her brown eyes toward black, made the purple half-moons beneath her eyes even darker.

"It's fine," Stella said. "Thank you."

Her voice sounded like a grandmother's, soft and sugar-sweet. In fact, everything about her screamed "grandmother": the half-sized glasses, the way she held onto the seatbelt with one bird-bone hand, the slow sighs that she didn't even know she was making. Still, she held herself straight up in her seat, not allowing her head to lean on the seat rest.

"Your mom bring the glasses?" he asked, to hear her speak instead of sigh.

Stella touched the earpiece as though she'd forgotten she had them on. "I rang a nurse," she said. She took the glasses off and folded them. "Had them brought up from the gift shop. My vision's gone haywire."

Stella had her head back at the window. He watched her while he drove. The disease had tightened her round face, made her cheekbones seem higher and larger. His instinct was to reach between the seats and take her hand. Reassure her: *They got it all, everything's fine.* But he couldn't stand to see her turn back toward him, to see her eyes hidden behind the lenses.

But she surprised him by reaching her hand out to his across the space. He took it, even though he needed to shift. He didn't understand much about what was happening or why, but he understood that you didn't waste time and you didn't turn down an extended hand. Her hand felt light and empty, a discarded crab shell.

With her other hand, Stella rubbed at something on the window. "I'm tired," she said. It seemed to be the beginning of a sentence. He waited, her hand lighter and lighter in his own. The only sound was the rev of the unshifted car and the squeak of Stella's finger against the window. These sounds stretched out so long he thought he might have misjudged, maybe there wasn't more she wanted to say. He let his foot farther off the gas—they were going 20 in a 40 now—and opened his mouth.

Stella tightened her fingers on his. "I'm tired," she said again. "But I was thinking …" she broke off, rubbed the window harder. A car came up behind them, blinked its lights. He shifted the wheel to the right, gave them space to go around. His ears felt like they were the only thing alive, listening for her.

She looked at him finally, gave him a smile that didn't show her teeth. Her fingers unraveled from his. "You should shift," she said. He did, and the car gave a grateful lurch ahead. They drove in silence the rest of the way home, Stella's soft-shell hands holding tight to her seatbelt.

That night, he was surprised when Stella got into bed next to him in only a T-shirt. He'd picked up *Cancer Husband*, and found it wasn't that bad, if a little froufrou for his taste. Of course, he'd started with the chapter on sex. Very vanilla, but still.

Stella reached out and took the book from his hands. She closed it without letting him mark his place and dropped it on the floor beside the bed.

"No more reading," she said.

Hearing her say that made him smile. She used to say that all the time, when she wanted his attention for cuddling, for sex. He rolled toward her. Her body took up less space now—still her, only smaller, as if she'd been slightly shrunk. Still the same curves, the waist that hollowed out toward her round hips. He felt huge next to her, a dangerous giant who might roll over and crush her.

He couldn't resist her play. He put his hand soft against her arm, slid it up beneath the shirt sleeve. Her skin was cool, but for the first time in a long time, her muscles didn't tighten in pain at his touch.

"No more reading?" he said. "Why, do you have something better for me to do?"

Stella put her nose against his neck, inhaled deep.

"I might be able to think of something," she said.

He swallowed hard, unable to speak. How does it feel when your wife comes on to you, finally, finally, after cancer? You feel like the earth has been out of axis, but you didn't notice, until just now, when everything rights itself and settles in, the way it's supposed to be.

"I've missed your body," she said. A sigh, but different from the sighs she'd made in the car. "I've missed *my* body."

How to say he'd missed her body too? He didn't know, so he answered with his fingers on the curve of her hip, followed the slimmed half-circle of her ass. No underwear. The crease where the bottom of her ass met her legs was soft and smooth. Just the feel of it made his hand ache to slap it.

He almost did slap her, but took his hand away, fisted it around the blanket. How could he even think of it? He didn't know, couldn't imagine what kind of person he was to want it the way he did.

Stella's lips moved smooth against his neck. She took his hand from the blankets, but laid it back on the edge of her hip, where her T-shirt met her skin.

"Undress me," she said.

She sat up, and he pulled her shirt off over her head. And there was her star, right above her right nipple, the red heat of it dulled. He wanted to put his finger on it, to lick it and taste it like sun-warmed earth. He thought it would burn his tongue.

He said, "Does it hurt?"

"Stop asking," she said, and her voice was brisk, but also tired.

He nodded. Even to himself, he'd started to sound like a quiz book. How are you? What do you need? How do you feel? It was as if he didn't know what to say when he wasn't asking about her. He searched for something about his own day that would be interesting to her. *I thought about fucking you the way we used to. I thought about clamping your nipples until you cried, until you could sleep and smile again.*

Stella put her own finger over the star, pressed harder than he would have thought.

"Sometimes it hurts," she said. "Not now."

She dropped her hands, put them on his hips.

"Anyway, I don't want to think about it," she said. "Can you just fuck me?"

Her voice was beyond Type A into bitter, a spit of bad tastes. It hardened his cock and made him nervous to touch her, at the same time. She closed her eyes and leaned her head back, exposing the full length of her soft, white neck, the pulse that talked to him there. He leaned into the pulse, put his lips against the thin blue line.

"Yes," he said. "I can fuck you."

But, then, he couldn't. He wanted to, he tried, but the star kept shining up at him off her skin, a beacon to remind him. Everything he did—his tongue at her pink nipples, avoiding the scar, his fingers down her pale belly, even the moment when, finally, he entered her, every ounce of him, his entire cock, inside her—at every moment he was making love, he was taking care. He didn't realize it at the time, he thought they were together in this slow, languid night. But right before he came, he opened his eyes and saw her looking somewhere else. Her body moved in the slow-motion rhythm he'd started, but her mouth made small noises of pain. He tried to rise up off her, but he was already coming, too late to stop, and his shudders made his "I'm sorry"s sound tinny and hollow, as if they were coming from light years away.

Stella didn't come on to him again. He wasn't surprised, but he still hoped for it, watched for her to take the lead when she felt okay, but there was nothing. She didn't even undress in front of him.

Within the week, Stella started work again, and they settled back into what he thought of, sadly, as their old rhythm: too much work-work and house-work, passing each other on the stairs or in the kitchen, hands full of laundry or dinner. He'd thought that once someone got sick, the way Stella had been sick, you didn't, couldn't, just go back to normal. That you never took life for granted, or passed each other in the hallway without touching.

He started masturbating in the shower. One hand on his cock, the other against the shower door, in case she came in to pee. He was embarrassed for himself, for his desire, but he didn't want to embarrass her, or make her feel worse. He used Stella's soap—it smelled of sage, which smelled of her—lathering it until he could slide his fist up and down. Although he tried to think of other things, his mind was all Stella, Stella in nipple clamps, her ass beneath the flat of his hand. Keeping quiet, coming with Stella in the house but without her, made his teeth ache and the bottom of his stomach clench up in cramps. And, still, he couldn't stop. The pain cleansed him somehow, made it safe for him to be around her.

But after two weeks, he couldn't stand not touching her anymore. He put his arms around her one morning while she was dressing and kissed the bare back of her neck. The smell of her sage soap and her curves against the fabric of her skirt made him press his hips into her ass, harder than he'd meant to.

Stella leaned against him, bare shoulder blades into his chest. She let her head fall back onto his shoulder, and he kissed the side of her mouth. He hadn't realized how much he'd missed her breath, minty and sweet.

"You'll make me late for work," she said against his lips.

"Do you care?" he asked.

She shook her head no, and he turned her toward him, pressed his mouth hard to hers. His hands followed her lower back down to her ass. He cupped his palms around her curves and pulled her hard against him.

Stella made a small cry into his mouth. Panic spread up through his chest. He let go of her body, stepped back.

"Jesus, Stella, I'm sorry," he said. But even in his panic over hurting her, he couldn't stop looking at her body. How her nipples were like stars too, a constellation against the sky of her chest. How her waist curved in and then swelled into hips. His cock twitched, sending a mixed flood of arousal and shame.

Worst husband of the year award, right here.

"Don't you dare," she said. Her voice was shaky, something he hadn't heard before. "Don't you fucking dare tell me one more time how sorry you are," she said.

He nodded. His body was heavy, heavy. His hands, his head, his cock shrinking against his thigh, everything held on the bed by this strange gravity. He vowed he would masturbate every day, he would take a lover if he had to. He would not ask any-thing more of Stella, of her body, than what she offered him.

Stella stepped closer to where he sat. And there was her star, shining with its red heat. He couldn't look away. Did his eyes feel pain? He thought they might.

"Touch it," she said.

But he couldn't until she took his wrist and brought his fin-gers to her skin. The star wasn't hot at all. It felt like Stella's skin, only more so. Thicker, tougher, with six small rays leading out. And she didn't flinch when he pushed a bit against the small points of it. Instead, he thought she might be leaning into him harder.

He pulled his finger away, looked down at it in his lap. Did the tip of it burn, or was it only his guilt that made the skin seem hot? He couldn't tell.

"I don't know what to do," he said.

Stella put her hands beneath her breasts, lifted them up, her nipples pink stars in their own right. His cock tried to stir, but stayed down beneath the weight of air.

"I need you—" Stella started, and then got down on her knees in front of him. There was no rug, and he worried about her knees on the hardwood, but she didn't seem to notice.

"I can only say this once," she said. "Maybe, maybe I can't say it at all."

When Stella tried not to cry, her nose pinkened at the edges.

It didn't happen often. He'd seen it once, maybe twice, since he'd known her. The splotches of pink made him happy, not because he wanted her to cry, but because he suddenly felt less alone in this thing that had happened.

Stella covered his hands with her own, then lifted her chin until her brown eyes looked right into his.

"I need you to stop fucking me like I'm dying," she said, and her lips moved fast, like she was afraid they would stop. "I'm not dying. But every time you touch me soft, every time you ask if I'm okay, another little piece of me falls off."

Something started within him, a pain he had not known. It began at the inside of his chest, flowed outward to his skin, his arms. His breath hitched and came ragged. He wondered if he was having a heart attack. He squeezed Stella's hands, and she squeezed back.

"Now," she said, "I'm going to walk out of the room, and when I come back, I need you to fuck me like I'm actually alive."

Then she stood and turned. Still stuck to the bed, unable to rise or move, he watched her walk out of the room, the strength of her bare back, the way her ass filled out her skirt. The star he couldn't see, but could still feel, not as heat, but as light, guiding him.

"Baby," she said and her voice was strong and sure from out in the hallway, "You're going to have to get out the crocs today."

At the sound of her voice, his body came free of the gravity that held it. He could raise his hands, stand. His cock, too, rose as high as it could beneath his jeans. Before she came back in, he pulled open the nightstand and dug the nipple clamps from beneath the stack of books they didn't need to read. He looked at the clamps in his hands, their pointy teeth, and remembered the contrast their silver shine made against Stella's skin. The way she sighed in release when he clamped them to her nipples. He smiled and slid the clamps beneath the pillow for later. Let her think he'd forgotten, let her wonder. He was the one in charge, after all.

She walked in, naked now, her star shining from its place on her chest. He moved toward her, following its light.

ON THE TWELFTH DAY...

Andrea Dale

Stacie's hands trembled as she untied the green ribbon that bound the Christmas present on her lap. Vince hid his smile, not wanting to distract her. They'd discussed this at length already, but knowing what was in the box—what it represented—was far more powerful than any conversation could ever be.

Just before she opened the box, she looked up at him, eyes seeking reassurance. Now he did smile, and cupped her face in his hands. The tree's multicolored lights made ever-changing patterns like stained glass on their skin.

"I love you," he said. Then his smile faded. "Open it."

She shivered at the tone of command in his voice.

"Oh...oh, Vince, it's beautiful," she breathed at her first sight of the red collar nestled in silver tissue paper. She caressed the soft leather, held it up to her throat.

"No." He took it from her hands. She was confused, and he wouldn't hold that against her. "It's mine to put on you," he explained. "You're giving me permission to do that—and to do whatever I want after it's locked around your pretty throat."

Stacie swallowed, but her gaze was steady. "Yes." And as he buckled it on her, she softly sang, "On the first day of Christmas, my true love gave to me…"

Twelve days. From Christmas Day through January sixth was the time she gave him to introduce her to BDSM, to guide her into submission, to give her the chance to decide whether this was what she wanted for their relationship.

He wanted it. But he loved her too much to give her up if she chose against it.

He loved that she was willing to try.

Day one, the collar. He let her get used to the sensation of wearing it, reminding her of her subservience. In real life, he wouldn't make her wear it all the time, nor would he expect her to wait on him hand and foot. But for this limited time, this learning experience, he sent her off to do the dishes, nudged her chin down if she looked directly at him, reinforced for her his expectations.

On the second day, he spanked her.

They'd played with that a little before, with her squirming and giggling. Now, though, she took it more seriously. When he laid her over his lap and told her not to move, he heard her sharp, indrawn breath.

One for each day, he informed her, and she was to count them off.

"One…sir," she said clearly. "Two, sir. Uh! Three. Three, sir!"

They came progressively harder, the air reverberating with the crack of his hand against the plump curve of her ass, which steadily reddened.

Dipping a hand between her thighs, he found how wet she was, and the knowledge made him instantly, painfully hard. He took her there on the floor so her tender flesh would rub against the carpet, heightening the sensations.

She sobbed and tensed so hard when she came, he thought she might break apart. But she clutched him, and he told her, unable to keep the pride from his voice, that she'd done very well, oh so very well.

He'd tied her hands with scarves before, so it was a natural progression to add light bondage for the third day. Fur-lined cuffs in a cheerful shade of purple, wrists and ankles. Face-up first, to toy with her nipples and nibble at her pale flesh until she begged—before she realized she wasn't supposed to do that. He was fascinated by the progression of emotions across her face: first shocked realization and guilt, then a level of fear, and then a second realization, not of what she'd done but that she'd be punished for it.

Although she fought to mask it, he definitely saw excitement. Anticipation.

He recuffed her facedown with a pillow under her hips and enjoyed her whimpers and squeals as he spanked her, swiftly and soundly.

He slid his cock between her and the pillow and waited while she struggled against the urge to grind her clit against the hard length of him.

When he finally slid into her, it was preceded by the warning not to come until he gave her permission.

He took pity on her and told her to come when he knew she was pitching over the edge anyway. But her writhing against his cock and his hand, her relieved and delighted screams, were all worth it.

Clamps adorned her pert breasts on day four. He was so fascinated, so turned on by the sight of the clamps pinching her sensitive nipples, making them pucker and darken, that he kept putting them on and removing them all day.

It was all he could not to pull out a tiny little whip from his locked box and flick it against her imprisoned buds.

No. Not yet. There was time for that later. But from the way she walked when wearing the clips, her chest thrust out just a little, gently, to increase the sensation, he guessed that she might not be averse to stronger stimulation in the future.

That night, he fastened the clamps so the connecting chain would reach her mouth, and he told her not to drop it, no matter what. It made the clips pull deliciously, and didn't allow her to howl her pleasure when he brought her to orgasm with his hands and mouth and cock. Which, he knew, was the hardest thing of all for her.

He pulled the clamps off at the very end, and her final, violent climax drove him over the edge with her.

On the fifth day, she grew more nervous. He'd been relatively gentle up until now.

Now, however, he started bringing out the harder stuff.

The spanking bench, which he strapped her to so she couldn't move even if she wanted to disobey him.

The spreader bar, which kept her legs apart and made it harder for her to come. He put a vibrator against her clit and watched her struggle as he stroked his cock. He was heady with need, heady with what he was doing with her and how she was taking it.

So close. So desperate. She would have turned her wide, blue eyes on him, pleading, if he hadn't blindfolded her.

He'd told her to come at will, but still she fought, the need to bring her legs together to assist her warring with her pitched arousal.

He was so close himself, it was hard to keep his voice steady and stern. "On the count of five," he said. "If you don't come on five, we'll stop, and you'll be punished."

She froze, taking in his words, and then he began. "One... two..."

She came, hard, on five. And so did he.

The sixth day was much the same, only with the addition of paddles and a crop to heighten the scenario. Between rounds, he asked for her honest opinion: what she liked, what she didn't like. She had yet to use her safeword, although she'd gasped "yellow" a few times so that he'd ease off.

Still, she slid her fingertips over the welts he'd raised, and her smile spoke volumes.

He didn't overdo it, because he didn't want her too sore for what he'd planned for day seven: New Year's Eve.

She'd been naïve enough to believe, when he told her to wear the panties with the remote-controlled vibrator in them, that they'd be having fun on the way to the club, or on the way home.

Not *at* the party.

"I'm going to make you come," he said.

"Here—now?" she gasped, and added, just in time, "Sir?"

"Yes. Right here. At this party."

He'd been delighted to discover this was one of her feared fantasies.

"But—"

"If you don't, I'll spank you right here, in front of everyone."

Which would be worse for her? He knew the choice inflamed her. He directed her to the dance floor, thumbed the control. The music pounded; nobody could hear the buzzing. He watched her shudder and cry out, her hips grinding to a beat only she could hear.

"Very good," he said when she returned to him, triumphant and flushed. "Now, for the next one..."

The butt plug the next day was another test for her, close to but—it turned out—not over her limit. She'd been willing to gently, carefully explore anal play before—just a finger, though, so the toy was another matter altogether. He positioned her on hands and knees, surrounded by well-placed mirrors so she could see the plug sticking out of her nether hole. The swirly green glass contrasted with her blushing skin.

She didn't want to look, but opened her eyes when he ordered her to. Kept them open even as they tried to flutter closed, while he quietly kept up a litany of description: How she looked. How the plug looked. How her ass looked. How hot and slutty she looked.

He didn't tell her that what he'd love to see was one of the plugs that sprouted a horsey tail or peacock feathers. One step at a time. Don't scare her. He kept up the controlled façade, wondering if she had any clue how his emotions raged. He warred between wanting to try everything, wanting to push her to flying ecstasy, and the knowledge that at the end of the twelve days, she might say no and end it all.

He ordered her on top of him, so he could watch in the mirrors.

She carefully took him in, adjusting to the sensation of having both holes stuffed. "Thank you, sir," she whispered, and he realized why when he found how wet she was.

It boded well for the following day, when he introduced his cock into her ass and watched her flesh pebble with goose bumps as he slowly thrust into her. She didn't come from that alone, but he spent a long time with paddles and vibrators and clamps afterward, rewarding her deep into the night.

Day ten. She was already relaxed and eager, her nipples puckered, when he blindfolded her and cuffed her arms over her head to a convenient hook in the beam.

Most days, he'd told her what her present was to be. Not today.

Today he wanted to catch her off guard.

He paced around her, caressing her as he spoke in soothing but controlling tones. When he had her aroused, pliable, he asked her if she'd do anything for him.

He wasn't surprised when she hesitated. Too soon. But he'd planted the seed. He told her that was okay, that he'd never go against her wishes.

"Anything I suggest, you can ask me to stop any time. They're just ideas until we implement them."

He grazed her nipples with fingers and teeth before adorning her upturned breasts with clips, the kind with little bells on the ends that chimed when he played with her.

"You like my hands on you, don't you? My mouth, my tongue. My cock." As he spoke the last, he rubbed the head of his penis against her slickness, along the hard bud of her clit.

She trembled in her bonds, the muscles in her arms tight as she clenched her fists. "Yes," she repeated in breathy little gasps. "Oh. Yes. Yes. Sir."

In a quick, careful motion, he replaced his cock with a dildo. One stroke with his cock, then one with the dildo, so she couldn't quite tell. He slipped the dildo into her pussy, gently fucking her with it, not enough pressure or speed to bring her to orgasm.

He did the same with a smaller one, well-lubed, slipping it

into her ass while he told her how good he felt there. She whimpered and agreed, far gone enough not to tell the difference.

Back and forth. One, then the other. Toying with the dildos, and the clamps on her breasts. She was disoriented, but in a good way, flying on the myriad forms of stimuli.

He lifted her—she was such a slight thing—and eased her onto his cock, her legs wrapped around his waist. Like last night, her pussy was so tight, the slim dildo in her ass pressing against the length of him.

She gave him so much. He didn't even feel the urge to drive into her, knowing he had to move carefully.

"How would it feel," he asked, his voice rough with passion, "to have *two* sets of hands on you? *Two* mouths, *two* cocks? *Two* men worshipping your body, inside you, all over you."

"I...think..." She took a deep breath. "I think I would...like that, sir."

"How do you know it's not happening right now?" he asked.

Time stopped. He felt her entire body go taut as her mind raced to assimilate the possibility. Even her orgasm seemed to come in slow motion. He was aware of it building inside her, gearing up like a tidal wave gathering strength and racing toward the shore.

When it crested, her convulsions sent him tumbling into the surf along with her.

He pushed her limits again the next day, along with again throwing her off guard, letting her believe things were happening that actually weren't. Perception was everything. The sight of the needle, long and slender, before he blindfolded her. The judicious words he chose, describing how beautiful she'd look with her nipples pierced. The careful application of an ice cube on her breast followed by the touch of a needle—never breaking the skin—although she didn't know that.

She knew only ecstasy.

Epiphany.

The sixth of January dawned glitteringly clear. Vince brought Stacie breakfast in bed, the French roast steaming, a single peach rose in a vase.

She was understandably confused, but at his urging she enjoyed the mushroom-and-Asagio omelet, the fresh fruit and croissant. He nibbled off her plate, having already eaten while he prepared the food.

When she was finished, she looked at him expectantly for the collar.

He shook his head, not even looking to where it sat on the night table. "For twelve days, I promised you gifts," he said. "And for twelve days, you promised to accept them."

She put her hand to her throat. "Have I not...?"

"No," he said quickly, taking both her hands in his. "You've been amazing. Perfect."

He took a deep breath. "Our agreement was twelve days. On this, the twelfth day, this is the gift I give you: me. Everything I've shown you, everywhere I've tried to take you. Understand this—I will always love you, always be with you, no matter what you decide, no matter if you decide that what we've explored isn't how you want to be.

"But I'm always here for you, and that's all I can give you, in whatever way you'll have me."

Her answer was simple. A sweet, dazzling smile, before she bowed her head and held out the collar to him.

THRILL RIDE

Matt Conklin

Dylan was a different kind of top, at least with Marie, the girl who'd finally gotten him to settle down after who even knew how many years of bachelorhood. With Dylan, it seemed like he'd been born a single man, a loner who could still manage to pull the hottest chicks, if he wanted to make the effort. When he finally did cast his eyes on a girl, she was his, hook, line, and sinker, and Marie had been reeled in in a big way. She'd fallen not for his charm, but for his mastery, his ability to read her desires before she could even form them. He was the first guy who could take her to those special places she truly needed to go.

He wasn't the guy you'd find in their suburban S/M club dressed head to toe in leather, holding a whip and trying to look mean while grabbing her by the collar and dragging her around, to the delight of the horny onlookers. He wasn't a rough-and-tumble master insisting that she bow before him and cater to his every whim. He was nothing like the stereotype of dominant men she'd come to believe was not so far from the truth. In fact, Dylan's greatest weapon was his mind, and what a sharply wicked instrument it was, conveniently hidden away, coming out only when he wanted to play.

From the outside, their lives couldn't have looked more normal. They each got up in the morning and commuted from their suburban New Jersey home into Manhattan, taking the bus to Port Authority and then to their jobs as a lawyer (his) and a furniture designer (hers). Neither bore any outward symbols of kinkiness, like some of the people they'd seen at the clubs they'd visited a few times; they never stayed long. She didn't wear a collar, in private or public. There was no secret letter, scarlet or otherwise, to be found anywhere on her body. She wasn't pierced anywhere but her ears, had no special nicknames or code words. In fact, some of her colleagues had been shocked when she'd gotten married; they'd had her pegged for an uptight, asexual bitch.

But that was their dirty little secret. Somehow, Manhattan, with all its decadence and sexual possibility, left them cold. They liked the commute, the escape back into a land where people had lawns and cars and kids, where life didn't revolve around status and money. He didn't want to compete over who had the biggest cock; he knew and liked his just fine, and was grateful that he and Marie had some space to focus on the important things in life—like his dick, and her worship of it. He wasn't one of those guys who think every girl's mouth is made for blow jobs, but he knew that with Marie, "making" her get on her knees was the magic ticket to getting her ready for whatever he might want to do to her. He'd never seen a girl so wet as she got after he shoved his cock in her face. Even just a whiff, a lick, a taste had her panting, begging, greedy for his touch.

He'd already done plenty of kinky things to her, and he had plenty more he wanted to try. He liked to find new and creative ways to make Marie collapse, at least inside, until her pussy was so tight with arousal she thought she might scream. When it came to topping, he was like a fashion maven who doesn't want to be seen in the same outfit twice. Once he'd played out a scene with Marie, his mind was racing to the next challenge, the next way to make her moan and cry out, to make her realize how glad she was to be with him and only him. He got goose bumps every time he managed to take her to that place.

His most recent test did make her scream, many times, some in excitement, some in fear, some in sheer amazement that she was actually doing what she was doing—all without his even touching her. He thought there should be some kind of medal for that, but he was happy to claim Marie as his prize.

He woke her up on her birthday by jangling a set of keys in her ear, the grating noise making her think of an alarm clock, even though she'd deliberately turned hers off, having taken the day off work. She looked up at him, startled, then felt that same frisson of arousal she experienced every morning since they'd gotten together, that slight hum of alarm and awe that had her soaking wet in seconds, before her brain had even processed that she was officially awake.

"What're those?" she mumbled, rolling over toward him, crashing into his solid, thick, male wall of a body. He felt his cock strain, longing to rub against her, to be inside her, but first she had a very important test to pass—her driver's test.

"They're keys...to your new car. Happy birthday, baby," he said, grinning from ear to ear.

She looked at him as if he were crazy. "But—but—but," she stammered. "It's my birthday, Dylan! Or did you forget that I absolutely hate cars, am petrified of driving, and don't even have a license?" She turned away from him angrily, losing her morning glow, and her arousal.

He climbed on top of her, using his weight to sink her onto

her back, his dick nudging between her legs. She looked up at him defiantly, her brows furrowed, hate stamped across every feature. He held the keys in front of her with one hand while a knee slammed against her bare cunt. He'd always loved that she slept naked every night, making it easy for him to know, by sight, smell, and taste, exactly when she was ready for him. His knee told him she was ready, despite her anger, or perhaps because of it.

"We're going for a ride, whether you like it or not, my sweet birthday girl," he said, jangling the keys annoyingly before her eyes. "And guess who's driving?"

The grin was back, and she swallowed hard. She hadn't driven a car since she was twenty, and that was fifteen years ago, when she'd had the accident. All she could remember was two and ten—and terror. Even before the car rammed her from behind, she'd been skittish, checking over her shoulder so many times she'd wound up having to go to a chiropractor. From then on, she'd told anyone she ever met that she hated cars, hated driving, preferred walking and biking and mass transit. She hid behind the environmental aspect even as she threw her bottles into the garbage, ignoring the recycling bin. For Marie, it was all about the fear.

And that's the kind of top Dylan was, the truly sadistic kind, one who knows how to wield his power as a secret weapon, one that can leap up and surprise even the most solid of relationships. He'd been waiting three years to have the money to buy her the car, one he knew she'd fall in love with, once she got over herself. Driving was too sacred to live forever in fear. But he also knew what fear could do. He'd seen the look in her eyes whenever he'd pushed her to try something she was apprehensive about. He'd seen her shut her eyes and go limp, surrendering as he poured hot wax all over her body, seen her flinch as the first drops hit her skin, then seen her, later, sigh when he'd gone through every candle in the house and had no more to offer. He'd seen her through countless challenges, sexual and otherwise, always pushing her further, for her sake, and his own.

He got up, looking down at his wife, who looked even more beautiful with every passing day. "I'll make us some breakfast. Be down in twenty minutes. Trust me, Marie, it'll be worth it. And it's your birthday, remember?" It wasn't those last words, so much as the way he said them, that made Marie blush. She got his meaning loud and clear: If she wanted her birthday spankings, the special ones he reserved for once a year, delivered with his special sadistic gloves, the ones that hurt like hell, she had to do this. She sighed, burying her head under the pillow, knowing that in truth she had no choice. Her pussy had already betrayed her, pounding a rhythm between her legs that no amount of finger fucking or vibrator play could quell. She could resist him all day, but her sex would be there to reminder her that she liked it when he told her what to do, got off when he fired out orders as if she was some mere underling, spasmed when he grabbed her roughly. Much as the successful city girl in her hated to admit it, she liked when he treated her like a doll, a thing, a toy. Not because she was any of those things—oh, no—but because he did it so well. Underneath every commanding word, like the shading of a font on a magazine cover, was love, pure love, the best way he could express it. It was as if she could hear the echo of what he meant beneath what he said. "Suck my cock, my little whore," followed by a fainter, "I love you." She was *his* little whore, always, forever, just like she'd sworn on her wedding day. And for him, and only for him, she'd do it, or at least would die trying.

She came downstairs in jeans and a T-shirt, her brand-new birthday panties already creamed. She tried to ignore the twin poundings of her heart and her cunt as she swallowed some corn flakes, chugging water to help them go down. He let her be, perusing the paper, waiting, until she looked up at him, her gaze firm and steady. "Okay." They walked outside, where she saw a gleaming red sports car waiting there. If it were Halloween, she'd be unsure if it was a trick or a treat. A chill traveled down her spine, and she looked back at him before walking forward, keys in hand. Part of her was curious, wanting to touch it, pet it, but she wondered if it was like a tiger in the zoo, calm and sweet but just waiting for her to get close before tearing her apart. But she knew Dylan was waiting and watching, that he'd be with her, so she kept going, slipping into the foreign car's driver's seat, looking around, touching each object as if she'd never seen such things before.

He settled himself into the passenger seat, a first in all their years together. She'd told him on their first date about how deathly afraid of cars she was, so he'd designated a crack-of-dawn drive in their sleepy town as the perfect time to get her behind the wheel. He could practically see her heart pounding as she alternately glared at him and stared ahead, steeling herself for what she was about to do. His cock was rock-hard, a fact he tried to hide from her, since she needed total concentration to do the job. Sensing her fear, along with her willingness to push through it—for him—got him hornier than he ever could've imagined. "Damn you, Dylan. What the fuck?" she muttered, more to herself than to him as she adjusted the seat. "It's been so long. If we die tragically, it'll be all your fault," she warned. "At least this has an airbag." He watched her like a hawk, trusting her implicitly. He felt a shiver run through him when she turned the key in the ignition. Had she exaggerated her lack of driving skills, the way she often complained about being too fat or some other perceived flaw that never really panned out?

She pretended to ignore him, but he knew as sure as he knew his name that she had to be dripping wet. He put his seat belt on but remained at the ready, his total focus on her. If she really needed him, he was right there. He could practically hear her heart beating—or was that his?—as she pulled out of their driveway, looking both ways before turning. She reminded him not of a teenager with a permit, but of a little kid propped up on phone books, taking a forbidden thrill-ride.

He let her go a few blocks on her own, watched her face morph from calm to panic to somewhere in between. Her eyes were darting all around as her feet tried not to twitch as she worked the unfamiliar pedals.

"Turn right here," he said, and she did, albeit jerking the car sharply as she rode the curb, entering an empty bank parking lot. "All the way over there, and park the car," he ordered. It was still early enough that the bank was hours from opening, and they'd only passed two cars on the way. She got the car vaguely into a spot, but precision didn't matter at the moment. She had done it. Marie took the key out of the ignition and then sank back against the seat, shutting her eyes and trembling with relief and amazement, tears pricking at her eyes. *The bastard!* she thought as she looked over at him, her nipples pressed firmly against her thin tank top. *Traitor,* she admonished as she looked down at her lap, silently berating her pussy for pulsating the entire ride. She was so turned on she could hardly breathe.

Finally, she looked up at her husband. "How did you...?" she got out, the question asking itself as she looked at him through a film of tears.

"I knew you could do it all along," he said, pulling her close for a hard kiss. "And that's just the start. Soon I'll have you driving into the city for work," he said, only half meaning it; Manhattan traffic was a bitch, even for him. But one stroke of his fingers against the wet denim between her thighs told him all he needed to know. He pressed his knuckles against her dampness.

"You looked so fucking sexy on the road," he groaned as he lifted her out of her seat and over to his. They'd christen the backseat later. For now, he wanted her close as could be. She straddled him, and he slid a hand down the tight back of her jeans, gripping her ass firmly.

"Really?" she asked hesitantly, still not quite believing it. Fifteen years of fear, gone, or at least diminished. She'd done it, she'd driven. A car. On the street. Without crashing. Somehow, her husband had given her the best present of all. Up until that point. She buried her head in his shoulder, unable to look at him any longer, far too overwhelmed with sensation. She'd loved him before, of course, but this—this was different. This was why she'd chosen him, why he made her swoon, why one word from his lips could send her to her knees.

He spanked her through her jeans, simple swats—there'd be time for the gloves later—the pain dulled by denim, before pushing them down, unzipping, and plunging inside her right there in the light. By then, they could hear the roar of an occasional car going by, and she knew they risked being caught. It would've been funny, if she'd had time to think about it, if her head, and her pussy, hadn't been stuffed to the brim with his cock, and his power, and his ferocity. She'd necked in cars, even fucked in a few, in high school, when she'd had no place else to go. They had a huge house, but chose to do it in a car, in daylight, hidden but easily exposed should anyone happen by.

She'd demurred on public displays of affection with everyone before Dylan, but he'd gotten her to do all kinds of things she'd always thought were for bad girls. He pushed her, much the way his dick was pushing inside her, always there to catch her should she ever stumble. As she leaned back against the dashboard, he pushed her shirt up, displaying her nipples, giving him access to her clit while she slithered against him, bucking and grinding as she came. He was her top, but he was also a gentleman, and he waited for her climax to peter out before shooting his own come deep inside her, the warm liquid finally calming her racing heart. Looking down on him from her dashboard perch, Marie realized that every day with Dylan was its own thrill ride. When they were done, she handed him the keys, more a symbolic gesture than anything else. She would start driving again, but he was the one who was navigating for both of them, which suited her just fine.

CATHERINE WHEN SHE BEGS

Jason Rubis

Catherine entered the dining room in nothing but her skin. Naked except for a string of pearls. I didn't stare, but it did shock me, just a little. I looked past her and, to the extent I was able, ignored her. She did nothing provocative, nothing you might expect from a naked woman. I did things with my fork and knife to the food on my plate, and once I glanced up at her husband. What else could I do?

"She is not invisible," Dr. Varabedian told me in his musical growl. He had shaken his handsome head at every one of the maid's offerings—salad, rolls, a kind of stew I understood was called a *tokany*. Apparently he wasn't hungry tonight. Only the wine had escaped his litany of refusal; a bottle had been opened and left discreetly at his elbow, and he was methodically emptying it, glass by glass. Taking his time about it.

"I mean that you can look at her if you like," he explained. "Catherine. Looking at her is permitted. She is here to be looked at." He smiled his sweet, lopsided smile. "It is why she is here with us. This way."

I ventured a glance, which Catherine met with a sweet, wholly unselfconscious smile, thrusting a hand under one small, globular breast and hefting it as though to say, *See? Isn't it pretty?* She lifted the breast so high that she was just able to dip her head down and lick the nipple with an outstretched tongue.

When I didn't respond, she licked it again, and then repeatedly, fervently, until it was stiff and pink and shining with her saliva and apparently made so sensitive that each touch of her own tongue made her shudder.

I smiled a ridiculous, insecure smile and turned my eyes emphatically back to my plate. I was twenty-one years old at the time, and very unsure of myself.

Dr. Varabedian had been very kind to me, as had Catherine. He was an important man in my world, a history professor at the university where I was a senior. Catherine taught undergraduate classes in French and Italian. Male students adored her; the girls either adored her mindlessly or hated her with that venom peculiar to women who instinctively sense a rival. But the boys watched their step around her every bit as carefully as the girls. Certainly there was nothing about Catherine that suggested passivity or a person who could easily be either manipulated or hurt. She was small and blonde, bone thin, possessed of that ferocious sophistication that European women seem to have had bred into their bones.

I had actually met Catherine first. Junior year I had been a TA in her Elementary Italian class. We had barely spoken, apart from what was necessary to coordinate the business of classes and exams. Then one day she had come up to my table in the graduate library and, after a few moments of reading over my shoulder, began gently correcting the translation from Tasso I had begun on my own time, offering alternate words and phrases

in such a light, humorous voice that I took no offense, though I
had already gained a reputation in the department as a neurotic,
rather brittle little bitch, much given to sudden tears. I was one
of her admirers from that moment on. Inevitably I became one
of the few girls who was graced with occasional invitations to
her home, to have dinner with her and her legendary husband.

Tonight was one such night.

"Are you a lesbian?"

Varabedian was all but slurping his wine now, but he asked
this question in a gentle voice, not at all disrespectfully. Still, I
wasn't prepared to give him anything but the truth.

"No," I said. "I'm not." He frowned into his wine. Apparently this was not what he had either expected or wanted to hear.

"You ask her," he told Catherine, in a voice that was not cold
or rude so much as unthinking, as though she were a trusted ser-
vant who might more effectively deal with an uppity tradesman.
He turned away from us, staring off into the air as though the
strains of Mozart filtering through the dining room were visible
to him, if only at the cost of great concentration and effort.

"You like women," Catherine told me. It wasn't phrased as
a question, and I somehow didn't dare contradict her. I just continued staring down at my plate. I didn't touch my fork. I knew
dinner was essentially over.

"I've been a very bad girl, you know," Catherine said suddenly, brightly, as though this were a perfectly normal opening
to after-dinner conversation. At that, something almost made me
get up and run for the door. I don't quite know why, any more
than I know now what it was that made me keep my seat.

I think it was the undercurrent of real excitement in Catherine's voice that did it. If there had been any hint that she was
speaking under duress, I would have run. But the confidential
way in which she said *bad girl,* the way her accent reasserted

itself in its enunciation, made it clear that her husband was not in any way forcing her. I had no doubt that if she stood up at that moment her small, naked hindquarters would leave a visible spot of wetness behind her on the seat.

Was it the fact that she was telling *me* that she was a bad girl that she found so exciting? Me in particular? Would any other girl have had the same effect on her? Would a man have done, as well?

I didn't know. I don't know. And I don't know what made me ask her, "How? Why?"

Catherine reached for my hand, with a smile that seemed simultaneously relieved and welcoming. I blushed, knowing—and this was a bit of a novelty for me, at that point in my life—that I had said the right thing for a change.

"I broke a plate," she told me. "It was Vahan's favorite, a... what is it? Not a plate...it was bigger..."

"A charger," Vahan put in, murmuring the word. "Charger is what such a plate is called." He took a final sip from his glass and set it firmly on the tablecloth and reached for his water-glass. The drinking, apparently, was also over. After a long drink, Vahan sat back, folding his largish, fine hands over his belly. Watching his wife talk to me.

"A charger, yes. A pretty one. Japanese. *Inari*." Catherine pronounced the last word with a careful surety that suggested she was reciting from memory. "He had bought it at a store in San Francisco. Not antique, not expensive, but he liked it. It had fish on it, blue fish. Carp. Koi, they call them. Not an expensive...charger. But Vahan was very fond of it, you see. And I broke it yesterday while I was dusting. Vahan was very displeased."

"All right," I said slowly, unsure of exactly where this story was going. I did understand that she was—not lying, exactly.

She was telling a story. There had been no charger with koi on it. Not now. Perhaps there had been one that her father had been very fond of when she was fourteen and clumsy. Perhaps there had been one in the young Vahan's home, and a clumsy maid.

"So, you see, I had to be spanked." Catherine said this crisply, with great assurance. She stood up for real then and turned so I could see her ass. I could see that there were faded welts on her round little cheeks.

I inhaled sharply. Somehow that had succeeded in exciting me. It might simply have been hearing someone as sophisticated as Catherine tell me she had to be spanked. *Had* to be. Spanked like a naughty child. I squirmed in my chair, hearing that.

"You spanked her?" I asked Dr. Varabedian, quite timidly.

"I bent her over my knee," Vahan said, emphatically. "And I beat her." It could not escape my notice that he said *beat* rather than *spank*, though I knew he meant the same thing. "She bawled like an infant."

I reached out and, somehow unable to help myself, touched Catherine's ass. She stiffened noticeably, inhaling so sharply that I pulled my hand back, afraid I had hurt her. But her reaction was from excitement, not pain; even I could recognize that. If anything, I had tickled her. I suddenly became aware of an intense, varied bouquet of smells from my hostess's body: sweat-slicked skin just peeled from the chair cushion; the fragrance peculiar to underarms and feet only recently unclothed, left too long without the prescribed unguents and soaps; the salt smell of excited cunt. I had never smelled another woman's pussy before. Catherine lifted her arms over her head and I could see her armpits were laden with damp curling hair, a shade of blonde darker by several degrees than that on her head.

"Touch her," Vahan told me, gently but with great assurance, the utter confidence that I would not throw a fit, scream, call a lawyer, or sue the university for harassment the following day.

I ran my fingertips over Catherine's ass, startled by the difference in texture between its native smoothness and the rough weals that her husband—or someone else?—had recently inflicted on her. With her arms still up and folded over her head, she whispered sharply, mumbling something in, I think, French rather than her native Italian. After a moment she put her hands down, reaching behind herself to pluck at my fingers with her own, but Vahan said something to her and she put her hands up again, bowing her head. She turned and looked at me. I remember that a little place between her breasts had gone rosy, blushing.

"You can go home, if you like," Vahan told me. "I will call you a cab, if you like. Or you can stay with us."

"What will you do" I asked, "if I stay?"

"Whatever I wish to do," Vahan said, not at all haughtily, but still with a raised eyebrow. He stood up, took another long swig of water, and came to me. He was a tall, dark man, handsome as you like, with a remarkably kind, intelligent face. The smile he wore did bad things to me. It struck me—rightly or wrongly—that he might not have worn a suit tonight if I hadn't come.

He took my wrists in his and, after a questioning glance at my eyes, briefly kissed my fingers.

"I will flog her, if I wish to do so. Tie her hands over her head so she stands as she is now. Put a bar between her legs—a spreader, it is called, so that she stands prisoner for me. I will push a hand between her legs, tease her cunt. Or go down and lick her there. Beat her. I will certainly beat her. I will make her cry very loudly. You have seen already that she is very passionate, but she is a silly creature. A toy. My toy. My little baby."

He said all of this in the most loving voice imaginable. Catherine muttered and whipped her head sharply to one side once, just after Vahan called her his little baby, so that her pearls made a little sharp rattle.

"And what'll I do while you do all that?" My voice was shaking, not with fear. I had already decided I wasn't leaving.

Vahan glanced at Catherine, who stood breathing slowly but deeply, her flat belly dimpling slightly with each breath.

"You will watch. Sit quietly. Perhaps I will have you kneel." He did not add *like a good girl,* but then he didn't need to, did he? "When Catherine nears her...climax, you will go on your knees and lick her. You will push a finger into her. Not her cunt, but her asshole. You will put it in as deeply as you can. I want her to feel it when you do that. Feel you fingering her dirty place. Her asshole. Feel your finger in there like a little cock. And when you do that, it will be my turn to watch."

"And you'll like that?" I asked Catherine, who only hung her head and smiled.

"She will beg for it," Vahan assured me. "And Catherine, when she begs, is very beautiful. Will you stay with us, then?"

He was still holding my fingers, and now he squeezed them, pulling them one by one as if demonstrating how to milk a cow.

"I'll stay," I told him. Something made me add, "But I'm not your slave."

"You are young," Vahan said gently, and turned to the sideboard. There were flowers strewn on it, and hidden among their reds and purples and fleshy whites were some things I had not noticed before: leather things with shining metal buckles, rubber things with shining bulbous tips.

"I will not tell you that everyone is a slave to something," he said, selecting a pair of handcuffs that he opened with a frown and a businesslike snap. "A slave to someone or something. But it is the truth, even though it sounds like a cliché, and is. Clichés are sometimes painfully true."

BRIANNA'S FIRE

Amanda Earl

Noah lifted his baton slightly, and the guest solo violinist raised her bow. He tapped the baton once more, and she played the opening to *Adagio for Strings*. With a sweep of Noah's hand, the cellist and pianist joined in, soon to be followed by the rest of the orchestra.

This was what he loved about conducting: the perfection of having gifted musicians follow his directions, and turning their individual sounds into one glorious piece of music, seducing the audience with his firm control.

The violinist opened up on stage. She put her entire body—mind and spirit—into that performance. Observing her release to the audience and to him excited Noah. Her music was haunting and sublime.

During rehearsals that week things had been very tense between Noah and the violinist. He had given her instruction, and she had refused.

"Just listen to this piece, Brianna. You're playing it as it's written. Let me hear your own interpretation. I know you can give me more."

"Maestro, I have tried. I have practiced, but this is the best I can do."

The two of them spent hours together after rehearsal, trying to perfect her technique. He brought in other interpretations of the performance, but it seemed as if she wasn't listening. Her ears took it in, but her mind and spirit did not.

"Brianna," he said late one night after the frustration was growing, "let's get a coffee."

They talked that night, for the first time. She told him all about her life in London, the boyfriend she'd left behind.

"He was so weak, Noah. He never seemed to make decisions or take control."

"Is that what you want then, Brianna—a man to control you?" Noah's voice grew husky.

Brianna lowered her eyes and blushed. "Sometimes I think that is exactly what I'm looking for." She looked directly into Noah's eyes and a shiver passed between the two of them.

Noah's pulse quickened. This wonderful, sensual woman, so intelligent and feisty...he imagined her just for one moment in his arms, then on her knees at his feet. His cock stirred as he looked back at her.

The room was silent except for the beating of his heart. He took her hand in his and turned it over.

"You have beautiful hands, Brianna. That's surprising in a violinist."

"I want them to be soft, Noah, not calloused. I want to be able to give gentle touches."

The next rehearsal went better. It was as if the sharing of secrets had brought Brianna out of her shell. She was less timid. When Noah told her to try something, she did so.

At the party afterward, he'd removed his bow tie and tuxedo jacket, and was sampling his favorite champagne when Brianna approached him. During rehearsal, she had worn casual clothes. He had definitely found her attractive. How could he not? She was beautiful: long red hair, cobalt-blue eyes, and soft pink lips. Her dress now looked elegant, yet feminine: black as ebony, but camouflaging softness within.

"Noah, I just wanted to thank you for tonight. I don't think I've ever performed so well."

"You're welcome, Brianna. Those late nights really paid off, didn't they?"

"I'm so glad to have had this opportunity to play for the orchestra...to play for you." Brianna's eyes were as dark as the Irish Sea in a storm. Noah smiled and took her hand, holding it for just one second longer than was appropriate.

"I was impressed by the way you were able to let yourself go, Brianna. Not all performers can do that."

Her pupils darkened and grew as she breathed in quickly, which showed Noah that he had aroused her. Noah allowed his own breathing to quicken, to show her that he too found her attractive. He was a firm believer in communication without words.

"Yes, Noah, perhaps you do bring out the best in me," Brianna said quietly.

"Why don't we get you a drink?"

"Thank you, Noah. I would love..." she hesitated, "I would love a very dry martini."

Her voice was mellifluous. She could have been a singer. He kept his eyes fixed firmly on hers. He'd already noticed the curve of her firm breasts through her dress, the nipples visible through the thin fabric, a slender waist, and soft, glowing skin. He breathed in her mesmerizing scent of violets.

He focused on Brianna for the rest of the evening, ignoring

fawning patrons and sycophantic orchestra staff. This woman was different, fascinating, funny. They developed a crackling dialogue of repartee, playfully arguing. When he advanced, she parried, often with a subtle flick of wit.

He had a knack for revealing a woman's secrets, getting her to confess all, but Brianna told him very little. He knew she was from Ireland, but had spent most of her life in England, training at the London Music School. She had just done a stint with the City of London Philharmonic, but changed the subject quickly when he asked why. Soon the evening had to come to an end, as they had an early rehearsal the next morning.

"Look, you can't say that Cirque du Soleil is just a mere circus act. It is so much more, Noah."

"Ah, Brianna, if I'd known it was so easy to entertain you, I'd have brought out my magic act."

"That sounds like a wonderful idea, Noah. I look forward to that, but in the meantime, admit that they are a very sensual troupe. Their performance is filled with beauty."

"Sorry, Brianna, I'm just not a circus fan. I'd rather go to a good opera than see a circus."

"Opera? The sound of a woman caterwauling in as many languages as can be squeezed into one piece of music? Oh please, Noah."

"Well, perhaps one day, you'll accompany me to *La Bohème*. You'll see sensuality and sadness beyond anything you've ever seen. I guarantee. If not, you can make me go with you to one of your circus freak shows."

"I'd like you to come with me to see Cirque du Soleil, Noah. I want to see the smile on your face when you realize I'm right."

"Let me escort you to your car," he said. "I think you and I would disagree on just about every subject." He walked her over to a dark green Citroën.

"It does seem that way, but I do enjoy debating with you,"

she said, and paused, as if she wanted to say more.

"And I, you. But wait until I've taken you to an opera—you'll be struck dumb by its beauty."

He knew at this point that, if he were inclined, he could have suggested he accompany her for a nightcap, which would ultimately lead to sex, but that wasn't his style. Brianna was more than just a casual romp, and anyway, one-night stands held little interest for him. He needed much more, and perhaps she was the one to provide it.

"Good night, Noah. I'll probably toss and turn, thinking of a reply to your last gambit."

"Have a good night, Brianna. I hope you sleep well. I'm looking forward to our continued debate."

Brianna smiled and got into her car. Noah walked away, the scent of violets lingering from their touch.

That night, Noah felt restless and impatient. He knew he had to calm himself. He decided to go to an old hangout, Cris et Chuchotements. It was a fetish club with regular BDSM nights. He no longer frequented these kinds of places. He was used to slaves who knew just what he needed, but with Brianna on his mind, he had to be very, very patient, and he needed release.

He walked through the golden door, greeting the doorman, who still remembered him as a regular visitor. Noah descended the red-lit staircase into the dungeon, his cock beginning to harden as he contemplated the night's surprises.

He walked into the salon.

"Noah, how wonderful!" said a woman in the back corner.

Noah greeted Magda, his first slave. She had long, golden hair. Her curvy, voluptuous body was wrapped tightly in a red corset and short skirt. He could see the curve of her divine ass. He remembered the red marks he used to leave there with his first whip.

"How can I help you, Noah?"

"I thought I'd sample the wares a bit. I need a distraction."

"Did you want one of the women for your use tonight, Noah?"

Noah looked at Magda, and thought about taking her again, but too much history had passed between them.

"Yes, Magda. And make her a tall redhead, would you?"

Magda left Noah to think about Brianna while he waited. Brianna had sought him out, and this always excited him. She didn't expect him to come running for her. He would never do that, but he was definitely interested in her. He thought about the ritual they were embarking on. It was more than a court-ship ritual. It was the dance of master and slave. He would not seduce her, she would come willingly, learn to understand and accept her own needs as a woman and a submissive.

Noah remembered the advice of his mentor, Lord Collum, who had an eye for detecting and drawing out submissiveness in a woman, and who taught Noah as much as he could during their training sessions.

"Noah, if you really pay attention to a woman, she will give you clues about herself, and her sexuality. Her own perfume of musk and spice indicates arousal."

"What about a submissive woman, Regent? How can I tell whether a woman will submit to me?"

"Noah, we've got a long way to go before you're ready for that. Lots of training, but here are a few indicators: Intelligence and honesty are certainly essential. She has to enjoy the roles and rituals that go along with putting her into sub space. And she has to communicate her feelings of discomfort and pain at all times. A submissive has to be a strong and self-confident woman."

"Isn't that a paradox?"

"Not at all. She has to be strong enough to be open, to push herself further. She has to be self-confident enough to know that yielding will not take away from her strength."

"But aren't I just commanding her, and she just obeying?"

"Well, yes and no. Once you have established trust, you can dominate her, but a submissive has to have good instincts. She has to learn whom to trust. Also, she must always make the decision to yield each time. You must never take her submission for granted."

Noah thought about Brianna, the way she'd responded to him. Being around a maestro exhilarated her, breathed life into her. A dominant could be the air to a submissive's fire. Noah already knew that he wanted to be the air to stoke her fire.

Magda brought in a very beautiful woman named Colleen. She had long, auburn hair, tied up in a bun with tendrils hanging down the back of her short, clingy black dress. She was a businesswoman who was paying dearly for the chance to be dominated for the night. He was happy to give her this fantasy. And she was just what he needed.

He took her down to the whipping post in the dungeon, and practiced his whipping skills on her. Did it turn him on to have a woman tied up and at his mercy, awaiting the strikes of his whip? Absolutely. But even though his cock was hard, this wasn't about sex. It was about control and limits. He had his own limits. He was careful with this woman, giving her what she wanted, and taking what he wanted in return. She had been quite the screamer when she came with the flogger handle inside her, her ass covered in red marks. He needed those marks on her ass. He needed her screams. He could have come inside her, but instead he let her show gratitude by taking him in her mouth and paying homage to his cock. It felt so good to have the redhead at his feet. He imagined Brianna there. He was going to find a way to put her there.

It was an exhausting yet exhilarating session, and all he wanted to do was get home to his bed afterward, despite Magda's attempts to persuade him to share a drink.

"Another time, Magda," he said, and left the club.

Finally he'd be able to sleep. As Noah got ready for bed, he imagined Brianna doing the same. He knew she'd be thinking about him as she disrobed. He'd planted the seed, but not too forcefully. He had not pressed to see her socially. It was up to her to come forward now.

Noah's dreams that night were full of the long, lithe Brianna. He heard her violin playing, the soundtrack of her release, in his dream. He placed a forest-green, crushed-leather collar around her tender neck. Her hair was braided with hemp rope. He had seated her in a chair, her nipples pointed forward. Noah affixed her ankles to the chair legs with the thin rope. She winced slightly as the cord bit into her soft flesh. This made her lean forward, and her breasts jut out even more. Noah caressed her arms before placing them behind her back and tying them together with softer flat rope.

A woman bound is one of the most sensuous things in the world. She is completely vulnerable. Noah took this vulnerability seriously. He would never violate the trust so freely offered by a submissive. Brianna's large eyes and parted mouth reflected her arousal.

He kept her mouth ungagged. As much as he enjoyed seeing a woman strain and moan against a gag, he wanted to hear that beautiful voice cry out when she came. He gently unrolled a purple silk scarf and tied it over Brianna's eyes, wrapping it loosely so that she remained unharmed. The idea was to heighten her sensations by restricting her vision.

Noah's cock hardened as he gazed down at Brianna's glistening and bound body, but he steadied himself to ensure that he maintained control. He counted his breathing to even it, causing his erection to calm down. He took a feather and teased it gently over Brianna's long neck, onto her collarbone. A frisson of goose bumps decorated her breasts, arms, and stomach. He allowed the feather to trace her nipples, which stiffened in response.

She was tied but still able to part her legs further. Noah noticed her open cunt glistening with the onset of her juices as she yielded to him like a slice of ripe melon. He slid the feather gently over her thighs, and then carefully pressed it against her clitoris, which tightened and swelled as the feather moved insistently against it. Brianna pushed her pelvis up and down in time to Noah's feather. He kept his rhythm on her clit, gently stimulating her, but not taking her over just yet.

"Open your legs, Brianna," Noah said.

He watched Brianna's legs part wider and wider, straining against the ropes. "Oh, God, Noah, I'm going to come."

"Wait, girl. Don't come yet," Noah said while continuing to gently tease her clit.

"Please," she begged.

Noah gently inserted his index finger into her open cunt. "Now move, Brianna. That's a good girl."

Noah watched as Brianna lifted her hips up and down and felt her suck his finger in deeper.

"Not so fast, girl."

Brianna slowed down. He inserted a second finger, and she moaned in frustration.

"Oh please, Noah," she cried out, and her teeth bit hard against her lip.

"Beg for me. Beg and I'll let you come, girl. Do it now."

"Please, Noah, I'll do anything you tell me. You can do anything you want to me, just please, oh please, sir, may I come?" Her words burst out in short, breathless sobs.

He knew exactly how far to push her. It excited him beyond belief to have this kind of power over a woman. It was time.

Noah whispered the words in Brianna's ear, "Yes, slave, that's right, you will do anything for me. And now you are going to come for me, Brianna, come for your master."

Noah watched as Brianna let go. Her body relaxed, but her cunt tightened up around his fingers. These were the words she'd needed. And he was the one to give them to her. He could provide this release for her. He was a strong wind, and she, the embers. Sparks and air mingled and culminated in flame. She came hard, her juices flowing over his hand.

He awoke from the dream completely aroused. In reality he knew that it would take much more than that to get Brianna to the stage where she would come on demand for him.

The phone beside his bed rang.

"Hello," he said, still out of breath from his dream.

"Noah," Brianna said, her voice clear and sexy first thing in the morning. "Would you like to have breakfast?"

Brianna had passed the first test.

CHRISTMAS WITH SUZY AND MARY

Mike Kimera

This will be the first Christmas that Mary and Suzy and I have spent together. I've been thinking about them all day. On the overcrowded flight home I feigned sleep and summoned images of the two of them—bound, beaten, and fucked into exhausted happiness—that made my cock pulse with anticipation at the thought of using them and watching them use each other.

I was in my forties and twice divorced before I came to terms with the dominant side of my sexuality. Mary claims that she knew my real nature the first time that she looked into my eyes.

We were in one of those clubs at the edge of town, where the young people lose themselves to the rhythms of music and stoke each other into a sexual frenzy. I was feeling old and out of place and was about to leave when I saw Mary.

She looked too young to be in such a place and too small and frail to be unprotected. Yet the emotion stirring in the pit of my belly was not paternal care but ravenous lust.

It wasn't the way she flicked her long red hair or the prominence of her nipples under the T-shirt that hugged her small breasts; it was her smile that snagged me. Her arms were above her head, her hands were grasping her own wrists, her eyes were closed, and she was smiling. There was a wickedness in that smile that called to me. It didn't so much move me toward her, it was more that I was pulled into the sexual-magnetic field that her smile generated.

When I was so close to her that I could have licked any part of her that I chose, her body started to jerk forward, then rest, then twist forward again. Although the music made it impossible for me to hear anything else, I could have sworn that with each twist she groaned.

She had my full attention. If I had been asked, there and then, what I wanted from her, my only reply could have been: "Everything."

She opened her eyes when I put my hands on her breasts and ran my thumbs across her nipples. It wasn't something I'd decided to do; it was something that I couldn't refrain from.

When she made eye-contact, everything stopped. I was more aware of the intensity of her gaze than I was of the heat of her young flesh. I swear I saw the moment when she reached her decision. Then I started to breathe again.

She let herself fall against me, wrapping her arms around my neck, pulling my head down and pushing up on tip-toe until her mouth was close to my ear.

"You've been looking for me," she said. "I knew that if I stood here and imagined being flogged and flogged and flogged, you would find me."

I had no idea, then, what she meant, but the image of her being flogged and the reality of her pressing against me was too much to bear. I came, right there on the dance floor.

With any other woman I might have apologized. With Mary,

a different part of my brain took over. I pulled one of her hands from my neck and placed it on the sticky mess at the front of my trousers. She closed her fingers around me possessively, and squeezed.

"Are you going to make me clean that up?" she asked, as her thumb traced my shaft. "Are you going to punish me on my knees with your cock in my mouth?" Her other hand slid down my back and pushed past my belt, on its way to my ass. "Are you going to..."

I didn't let her finish. I grabbed both her arms and pushed her to her knees in one swift movement. Then I put my hand on the back of her head, wrapped some of her hair in my fist, and pushed her face up against my crotch.

She licked me through my trousers. She closed her mouth around my bulge and sucked. When she reached for my zipper with her teeth, I pulled her head back by her hair and we made eye-contact for a second time.

"Not until I give you permission," I said.

I could hardly believe I'd said that. What the hell did I think I was doing? What if she cried rape? What if she punched me in the balls? What if...

"Yes, sir. Sorry, sir." she said.

Her smile was still there, but there was a hunger in her eyes now that reflected my own.

I took her home and our journey began. That was almost a year ago. She's still here. For that, I am profoundly grateful.

Does gratitude sound odd on the lips of a self-confessed dominant? It should not. Don't be distracted by the fact that I am old enough to be her father and strong enough to leave her tight little ass covered in welts that write out my lust in a pain-drenched Braille; Mary is my equal as well as my slave. I realize now that the most important parts of my life have been written in an invisible ink that can be read only by the heat of our mutual desire.

In the time we've spent together, I've grown to know Mary the way that a sailor knows the sea. It is not that I understand her, it's more that I observe her closely and try to read the signs and portents that predict her actions.

Mary meets me at the door to welcome me home from my business trip to India. This time her intentions are not at all hard to read. Mary is wearing only a Santa hat, a red leather collar with matching cuffs, and novelty panties with "Ho Ho Hole" printed in white on a red background.

It's good to be home for the holidays.

Perhaps it is the way her nipples jut upward or the grin that won't quite go away even when she kisses me, but I know there is something Mary wants to show me.

I push her to her knees and let her unzip me and kiss me for the second time. She is diligent but, even with her mouth full, her eyes are pleading for us to move on to the next thing. Given Suzy's failure to greet me, I have my suspicions about what Mary has in mind.

When I am nicely hard, I say, "Okay, show me."

She is up off her knees so fast my cock is left bobbing in her wake.

"We prepared something special for you," she says and then leads me by the cock towards the playroom.

When I am away, Mary takes charge, even though Suzy is more than ten years older than her.

Mary was always proud of her bisexuality. She brought women to our bed with the same strut of achievement with which my cat used to drop dead birds at my feet: part tribute, part taunt, all instinct. But when Mary "recruited" Suzy to our household, she moved into conscious choice. The two of them are perfect together. Where Mary rushes gleefully toward submission, Suzy wrestles with it, needing to be bound and beaten before she can give herself up to the lust inside her.

Mary was Suzy's first female lover. Suzy had spent ten years in a sexless marriage, only to be dumped for a trophy wife once her husband made partner at his law firm. Mary discovered Suzy at a singles bar, took one look at her rounded figure and her wounded eyes, and knew she had to taste her. She followed her to the bathroom, where Suzy was adjusting her makeup in the mirror. She waited until Suzy looked at her, then she stepped out of the flimsy little dress she was wearing, stood naked, hands on hips, and said, "Want some?"

Suzy froze. Mary stepped up behind her, pressed herself up against Suzy's back, and firmly took possession of Suzy's breasts. When Suzy closed her eyes and groaned, Mary let go and stepped away.

"If you want me, follow me," she said, as Suzy turned to her, confused and breathless. Mary walked into a stall. Suzy followed.

On many occasions they've acted out for me what happened next, once even in the same bathroom at the bar. Mary wasn't gentle: she bit and slapped and pushed her small fist in deep. Suzy took it all and cried only from relief at her too-long-delayed release.

Now Suzy has two loves in her life, Mary and pain.

To my surprise, I've turned out to be good at pain. Before I met Mary, I'd never hit a woman. In fact, as an adult, I'd never hit anyone. I regarded myself as a civilized man with too much intellect to need to resort to violence. I still think of myself that way. Pain, the kind of pain I inflict, has nothing to do with violence. It has to do with strength and courage and the need to break away from the limits of the flesh.

The first time I hit Mary, I was in a kind of trance. She was bent over a chair, naked, butt in the air, an improvised gag in her mouth, and she wanted me to hurt her. I suppose I could have just spanked her, but at the time it seemed natural to use my belt. I remember the sound it made as I pulled it off my jeans, the weight of it in my hand when I bent it over, the noise it made as it whistled through the air. But most of all I remember that first impact. It was as if I'd jumped off a cliff and, instead of falling, had discovered I could fly. I felt powerful and purposeful and connected to Mary more intimately than I would have thought possible.

I've learnt a lot about pain since then: how to set a rhythm, how to raise and lower intensity, how to take Mary to the point where she cannot keep still, where she has to stamp her feet to earth the pain.

Mary likes pain as an extra spice added to the joy she gets from being tied up and used. For Suzy, the pain is the main event. She struggles against it, trying to subdue it, trying to make it go away, but she wants to be pushed and pushed until she has no will left to struggle with and can give herself up completely to the heat flowing through her.

I've grown fond of Suzy. She doesn't twist my guts as Mary does, but she has an enormous capacity for pain-induced pleasure and she will do anything that Mary asks of her.

Although Mary and I often play alone, I have never taken Suzy without Mary's participation. It is an unwritten rule that shapes the angles of the triangle we make.

When we reach the playroom, Mary skips ahead, stands triumphantly beside Suzy, points at her and says, "I wrapped your present."

Suzy does indeed look like a Christmas present. She is strapped, spread-eagled, on our St. Andrew's cross and tinsel trims have been added to the leather that binds her. A Christmas tree bauble hangs from the ring that Mary installed through Suzy's heavily hooded clit. Above the ring, Suzy's pubes have been freshly shaved and the words "Merry Christmas" have been painted in Mary's small, precise handwriting.

I move to kiss Suzy hello, looking forward to the weight of her breasts in my hands, when Mary says, "Do you want to see what we bought for you to open your present with?"

I'm intrigued. Mary grins, reaches down to a box beside the cross, and produces two silver metal eggs, so large she can barely fit them in her small palms.

I raise an eyebrow. Mary bends and slides the first egg into Suzy's cunt. "They vibrate, don't they, Suzy?"

"God, yes," Suzy says, then grunts as the second egg is pushed up her well-lubed ass.

"But the best thing," Mary says, reaching back into the box and pulling something out, "is the remote control."

I take the remote from her. It has two controls—one for each egg, I assume—that can be set at low, medium, or high. Mary drops back to her knees as I examine the remote, and rubs my cock against her face to keep me hard.

"Tell him what happens when they're both set on high, Suzy," Mary says, then sucks my balls into her mouth.

Suzy eyes flick hungrily across the remote as she speaks. "They vibrate against each other and I die and go to heaven."

I can take a hint as well as the next man. But I like to add a twist. I pull Mary to her feet, lead her across to Suzy, push her head onto Suzy's left breast, and tell her to suck.

Suzy is groaning by the time I finally kiss her hello and run my hand over her belly, but her eyes are still on the remote.

I set both controls to low. Suzy pouts at me. I push them both to high and her eyes widen. I can hear the eggs buzzing away.

The bauble on Suzy's clit ring starts to bounce. Mary is still sucking but has slipped a finger or two inside herself.

I know exactly what she needs.

It takes me a few seconds to find a condom to slip over the small remote. I show it theatrically to Suzy, then I push it into Mary's cunt.

"That's not coming out until I've come in her ass," I say.

Suzy barely registers my words. Her eyes are glazed and her head is rolling from side to side. They really were very big eggs.

Mary bends over and positions herself so that her head rests on Suzy's belly, her arms are wrapped around where Suzy's waist used to be, and her legs are braced and spread wide.

As I part Mary's buttocks and press home, I grin at the thought that this is going to be my best Christmas ever. Then I make a silent prayer to the universe that I will survive until New Year's.

RECLAIMING

Teresa Noelle Roberts

I set Deirdre's suitcases down, then shut the door behind us.

"Take off your clothes," I told her. "You're home now. And mine."

I watched several expressions fleet over Deirdre's beautiful face. First, the relief at being home after her long business trip (almost three weeks in Singapore, and then a stop in the Chicago office that morning for a meeting before flying home). The second, confusion, as she began to change gears from Deirdre McCarthy, kick-ass businesswoman, to my Deirdre, my slave.

Finally, the melting, the yielding, the surge of raw need. I saw it in her gray eyes, saw it in the speed with which first the coat, then the suit jacket, came off, and everything else followed.

Usually I meet her at the airport and start the transition from one mind-set to the other almost immediately—nipple clips to put on in the airport bathroom, vibrator just teasing at her clit all the way home, or maybe clothespins on her labia—but the way her flight worked out this time, I couldn't get anyone to cover my noon class and she'd had to take a cab.

I'd texted her before she got on the plane, though. As clothes went flying—blouse, bra, skirt—I could see she'd followed my instructions.

No panties. A small weight (a dangly earring we'd modified for the purpose) on the ring through her clit hood to tease at her during the flight. And freshly shaved, which I hadn't reminded her to do, confident that she'd take care of it herself, reminder or no.

She was a good girl, even when we'd been apart way too long.

"Do you need to use the bathroom?" I asked her.

"I went at the airport." The pause was a beat too long before she added, "Master," and I could see her eyes go wider as she caught herself in the near-error.

I wasn't angry.

In fact, I felt my cock twitch, stir, perk up more from its definitely-interested-but-not-hard-yet state.

Sure, I have a mental image of a perfect slave, one who never slips up, never rebels, never is anything except 100 percent submissive. But what gets me going, gets me hard, is taking a girl to that point, training her, breaking her in ways we both enjoy, then putting her back together so she's both stronger and softer than before. Repeatedly. Because perfection doesn't happen in the real world, and it would be pretty boring anyway.

The problem, if you want to call it that, is that my Deirdre's a true Type A personality. She strives for excellence in everything she does, which is why she was chosen to go to Singapore to straighten out a multimillion-dollar potential disaster. She applies that perfectionism to being a slave, as well.

And that leaves me well served, well fucked, and well loved, but without a lot to do.

But after three weeks of having to be Ms. Kicker-of-International-Corporate-Butt, she was understandably finding it challenging to slip back into her slave role.

And I was glad.

Glad in a way that started in my brain, pumped through my veins, and went right down to my toes, but definitely expressed itself through my cock, which jumped to attention at the idea of administering a reminder.

I grabbed her hair and pulled her into me.

A hard kiss. It wasn't the first kiss I'd given her in the few minutes she'd been home, but the others—on the stoop, in front of the cabby and the neighbors—were tame in comparison. This was the way predators would kiss if they did such things: tongue, teeth, a sense of barely restrained violence, as if I was trying to kiss through her skin and down to her bones. She opened for me, melted, then something seemed to click and she went from passively enjoying the kiss to giving back as good as she was getting, tearing into me like I was into her.

I liked it. I liked it a lot, her tongue dancing in my mouth, her naked body grinding against my still-clothed one. But she's supposed to wait for a signal from me before letting loose that way, in case I'm in a mood for her to lie back and wait, to be a passive object I pose and mold. (I wasn't, at the moment, but that was not the point. The point was her forgetting her place for a second.)

Fingers tangled in her short, dark hair, I pulled her head back, forcing her to look up and into my eyes. "Who do you belong to?" I asked. Demanded, really.

"You, Master," she said. But it wasn't convincing enough. She sounded thoroughly kissed, thoroughly hot and bothered, and ready for anything as long as it got her to the sex she must've been craving even more desperately than I was. (At least I could jerk off while she's gone. Unless she'd been bending the rules, and I doubted it, she didn't even have that pleasure.) But that's not the same as believing, deep in her bones, that she's my property, to treat her as I like, within reason.

She knows it. But right then, she didn't really believe it.

I could prove it, as I'd originally planned, by a teasing, protracted blending of pain and pleasure. I could prove it by taking her now purely for my own gratification, pushing her to her knees, using her hot little mouth, then telling her to unpack and take the nap she probably needed. (I'd make it up to her later—I enjoy making her scream with pleasure far too much to deprive her for long—but using her like that does get the point across.)

But I had a different idea.

I let go of her hair, shoving her gently away. "Upstairs," I ordered. "Now. Take the weight off your ring. And use the bathroom. I may not be letting you up for a while."

As soon as we could manage it, I was as naked as Deirdre was, and Deirdre was on her back, spread-eagled on our bed, cuffs holding her in place, their burgundy leather looking striking against her fair skin. Her eyes were wide, her pussy was glistening, and she was giggling in that way she does sometimes, half excited and half nervous. I'm sure she was expecting something more along the lines of the original plan, riding crop and knotted cat-o'-nine-tails and perhaps the singletail, toys and clamps, pleasure and pain building to an orchestrated crescendo that would bring her to orgasm and tears simultaneously.

Later. Tomorrow, or maybe later this evening, after a nap and dinner. We had time.

Now, though, I stood at the end of the bed and took one of her feet in my hand. I'm not a foot freak, but she does have pretty feet—movie-vixen-red toenails, soft skin, high arches. Gently, at least at first, I massaged the foot, even working my fingers

under the cuffs a little to get at the Achilles tendon. As I expected, I was rewarded with sighs. When Deirdre's in the business
world, she wears heels a lot.

When she seemed sufficiently melted, I went to work on the
other foot.

When I was pretty sure her brain was as far away as it had
been when she was half a world away, I casually asked, "Whose
foot is this?"

She giggled, either because it seemed like a ridiculous question or because what I was doing at that second tickled. So I
repeated the question, a little more forcefully, running my nails
down her instep.

So lovely, seeing her muscles tense and shift under her smooth,
gleaming skin at the stronger sensation.

This time she got it. "It's my foot," she said slowly, "but it
belongs to you."

If you don't live the way we do, that may sound like crazy
talk—but the words were what I wanted to hear.

It took longer than I would have liked. But it was the correct
answer, so I rewarded her by sucking and nibbling on her pretty
toes, kissing her arches, occasionally digging in with my knuckles against the fleshy parts to give a jolt of stronger sensation.

Seems she wasn't the only one who needed a refresher. I'd
forgotten, if I'd ever known, how much she liked having her feet
played with. She squirmed and giggled and moaned and made
little pleading noises. I knew they were pleas for stepping up the
action, for moving my kisses up her leg, but I chose to take them
as pleas to continue what I was doing.

I liked looking up and seeing her spread open, her pussy
lips slick and swollen and oozing honey, her clit so stiff that
the shiny titanium ring stood at attention, her cunt occasionally
pulsing from need.

My dick was pulsing too, eager to enter her, to sense my slave's more-than-willing body moving under me, to feel her cunt convulse around me until I exploded.

We doms are always reminding our slaves that they need to be patient. But that's a lesson that goes both ways. In the state I was in, I wouldn't last long once I was inside Deirdre, and I had a point to make before I could do that.

So I made myself be patient and worked on her feet for a while longer, until I think both of us were ready to lose our minds.

"Whose feet are these?" I asked her again.

And this time Deirdre answered without hesitation, "Yours, Master."

With that, I kissed and bit my way up her right leg.

Slowly.

Lavishing attention on all of it, not just the obvious places like the back of her knee and the exquisitely sensitive skin of her inner thigh, but the bits I usually ignore: her shinbone; the lovely, rounded swell of her calf muscle; her knobby knees.

"Whose leg is this?" I asked, just before I pressed my lips into the hollow at the top of her thigh.

"Yours, Master." Her voice was shaky with need and hope, hope that I would move from there to her aching clit.

I didn't. I licked away some of the glistening juices that had dripped onto her thigh, spent a little while glorying in the rich, musky smell of her arousal. Then I moved to her other leg and reclaimed that one in the same slow, painstaking way.

This time, I left bite marks on her thighs. And this time when I asked my question, her "Yours, Master," was a growl. Her body arched as she said it, opening her legs even more, pressing her hips against the air as she had against me, and I could tell that even a slight touch between her legs would bring her off.

I couldn't promise it wouldn't bring me off too. Just feeling her sweet clit and pussy under my lips and fingers, seeing and hearing her convulse in orgasm, was about to push me over the edge.

My whole body felt hard and sensitive as my cock—and that included places like my elbows. Even my hair felt as if it was on fire, sensitized as the air moved over it.

And if I felt like that, I could only imagine how my poor, lucky slave felt, teased like this after a few weeks without even the solace of her own fingers.

Just what I wanted.

So I continued working my way up her sweet body.

I took possession of her hipbones.

Her belly, that soft little curve between her belly button and her mound, the one she hated and I adored.

Belly button, upper abs, ribs. All mine.

The valley between her breasts. Definitely mine, and I played with fire to brush my cock there until we were both trembling and I had to resort to thinking about something, anything, else. (*Monty Python* routines. Dinner options. Whether I'd paid the cable bill yet.)

Neck. First my hand, gentle but firm, across her throat. "Mine," I growled. "Even your breath is mine." The other hand over her mouth and nose for just a second. No more than that, but she convulsed as if she was about to come. Light nibbles and nips where the skin showed in business clothes, and a hard, claiming bite where it wouldn't. Mine. Definitely mine.

Shoulders. Biceps and triceps. The sensitive inside of her elbows. The more delicate muscles of her forearms.

Fingers. Here I slowed down even more, sucking, nibbling, reducing her to incoherent pleas.

God, how I wanted to take those spit-slicked fingers and

wrap them around my cock, order her to jerk me off—not that I thought she'd need an order to get the idea, but we'd both get even hotter from my saying it.

I took a deep breath, counted to ten.

Then worked back up her arm and down, down to her breast.

Hovered there. Sunk my teeth in. Teeth and tongue and lips all working on her pink, swollen nipple, and this time, "Yours, Master" bubbled from her lips unprompted. "Yoursyoursyours" as her hips thrust up and her eyes glazed over, and she came.

Sweet Jesus, I don't think I'd ever seen her come before without being touched, somehow, between the legs. Close, sure, like she'd been with my hand on her throat, but not actually going over the edge without a cock inside her or fingers, a tongue, or a toy on her clit.

That did it.

I positioned myself between her legs.

I slid my eager cock over her cunt lips, still twitching from orgasm.

"Please," she begged. "Please, Master."

Her beautiful face was red, twisted with a combination of pleasure and need. Barely human, and utterly gorgeous.

"Whose cunt is this?" I demanded.

"Yours, Master."

"And what should I do with my cunt?"

This was hard for her, most of the time. Even after a few years together, she still had trouble making herself say the words—and at the moment, saying much of anything coherent had to be hard. (I knew. I was having a little trouble myself.)

"Please...please..." A deep breath, and her eyes got even wider, her pupils so dilated that black ate almost all the gray. "Please, Master. Fuck your cunt."

I was inside her before she got the words out.

No need for subtlety and patience anymore. I was pounding, fucking her hard, biting wherever I could reach as I did, glorying in her heated, musky smell, her wetness, her reactions, the fact that she belonged to me as much as one person really can belong to another.

I felt the second orgasm roar through her, felt it, I think, almost before she did, or at least before she started screaming.

"Good slave. Very...good...slave."

There was so much I wanted to say—that she was beautiful, and more beautiful than ever with her face twisted with passion; that I loved her; that I'd missed her terribly; that I was proud of her for being able to move between her two worlds and be so amazingly good at both roles; that I was the luckiest damn man in the universe just to have her in my life, let alone as my slave. And again, that I loved her and always would.

But the brain–tongue connection wasn't working right. I could form the sentences in my head, but all my tongue wanted to do was taste Deirdre's skin and make the occasional rabid-animal noise.

My whole body felt like a cock, and my cock felt like a volcano about to erupt, and Deirdre was coming again, or maybe still coming, around me, and I tried desperately to hold off a little longer.

Then she screamed "Yours!" and contracted even harder around me, like an orgasm inside her orgasm, and I couldn't possibly stop this time.

Hips jerking, everything else frozen by the force of what was pouring through me, I threw my head back and howled.

And somewhere in the howl were words, awkwardly choked out: "My slave. Always. Never forget."

I collapsed, or just about, using the last vestige of control not to let my weight go and crush her. I cuddled her for a minute or two in that position, then forced my brain into gear long enough to undo the cuffs.

I lay down next to her, gathered her into my arms. "Welcome home, beloved slave," I said, surprised how hoarse my voice sounded. Not so much from the shouting at the end, although that probably had something to do with it. More as if I was holding back tears.

"It's good to be home, Master." Deirdre's voice was hoarse, too, and suddenly she *was* crying. Smiling—grinning dreamily, like a well-fucked slave should be—but crying as well. "I can't give up work, and that means going away sometimes. I need that too, need to use that part of my brain. But you're my home and I'm glad to be back."

And I kissed her tears away until we both dozed off, my slave girl cradled in my arms where she belonged.

Mine. Home at last. And not likely to forget anytime soon where she belonged, or to whom.

LATE FOR A SPANKING

Rachel Kramer Bussel

Laura is late. There's no escaping the fact that the clock tower outside my apartment has just loudly chimed six and my spankee has yet to show. I walk around my bedroom, running my fingers over the implements I've set out in preparation. There's a tiny slapper, a small, patent-leather nothing of a toy, one whose bark will always be worse than its bite. There's a ruler, an extra-long, coated one, for maximum impact. There's a shiny black paddle, stern and strong, like me. There's one with fur on one side, for when I want to soothe her, or just lull her into a false sense of security. There's also a strap, my belt, a wooden paddle. I probably won't use them all on her, but I like to have them ready, just in case.

I pace around, trying not to get too angry. Our spanking dates are about fun, about mutual enjoyment as she bends herself over my knee or splays herself across my lap. Sometimes I sit in a chair, fully clothed, while she strips before me and then lies down, her long, black hair brushing the floor. I have to wait for her to become totally still. She's that perfect blend of nervous and excited that makes her body gently hum and quiver.

I pick up the strap and slap it against my hand. The noise and sting bring me back to Earth. I look at the clock and see that another ten minutes have passed. We've talked about this countless times; I've tried to instill in her the importance of punctuality, not only when she's meeting me, but generally. It's rude to be late, it insults the person you're meeting by prioritizing your schedule over theirs. She always nods contritely, and I give in to her, even though once I almost sent her home without her dear spanking. My cock was pleading with me to go through with it, though, and I did, though the lesson might've sunk in more had I been a stronger man.

My dates with Laura are about spanking and spanking only. You see, even though I'm dominant to the core, I'm in love with a sassy, whip-smart submissive named Evangeline. She knows she's got me wrapped around one of her tiny, delicate little fingers, and I actually like it that way. On the surface, I call all the shots, telling her when she can and can't wear panties, supervising her nipple piercings, exerting control whenever and wherever I can. I know it makes her wet when I give even the slightest command. "Spread your legs farther apart," I'll whisper in her ear on a crowded subway train. She'll turn and give me an infuriated, but utterly aroused, grin as she does it. She's only playing at being mad because now her panties will be wet, her pussy seething, her mind racing for the rest of the day as she wonders what else I'll tell her to do later that night.

We have an open relationship, but the door isn't flung all the way wide. We keep it partly cracked, just ajar enough so other women, like Laura, can get in and get the spankings and punishments they and I both crave. But, horny as they make me, Evangeline has forbidden me from fucking them. I've managed to work that energy and want into my scenes, even though it's sometimes hard to resist those wet pussy lips I'm not allowed to stroke or enter. Laura's the worst of all, the biggest temptation, and sometimes she gets spanked extra hard because otherwise I simply don't know what to do with all the pent-up arousal. Evangeline wins too because when she comes over after I've played with Laura, I fuck her so hard she can feel it for days afterward.

I finally sit down on the bed, my hand lightly resting on my crotch. There's no real way to simulate spanking a pretty, willing, needy girl's ass when you're by yourself. Watching videos doesn't quite do it for me; I need flesh and blood, I need to hear her beg, I need to look down at her face and see the answers written across her features. At six forty-five, my doorbell finally rings. I have to admit, I've pretty much given up on her ever showing up. Maybe we'll never see each other again, and while I'll be disappointed, what can I do? So I'm partly surprised, partly aroused, and partly annoyed when I open the door to see her standing there blowing her sweaty bangs up off her face, looking contrite and bedraggled but still goddamn sexy. She's pushing thirty but dresses like a schoolgirl—literally. She has on a pleated plaid skirt, strategically ripped fishnets, big black platform shoes, and a skimpy little white tank top and no bra, letting anyone who cares to look see the twin barbell piercings adorning her nipples. Her hair is in two braids, black eye make-up smeared around her eyes, red lipstick emblazoned across her mouth. Those lips are so tempting, even more than her ass; I've had many a fantasy about sinking my cock between them, letting her do what I'm sure she's brilliant at.

Just the way she makes her sorry face, her mouth open, eyebrows up, hip cocked, makes me want to fuck her. Since I can't do that, I let my annoyance show. "What took you so long?" I snap, blocking her entrance with my body, even though part of me longs to grab her and give her a hard, solid kiss.

"The train was delayed, and I forgot something in the house..." she replies. She seems to be making excuses, her voice getting whiny. When she looks up at me, her eyes blaze both apology and defiance. I know she hasn't been deliberately late so that I'd spank her harder; we don't need to play those kinds of reverse psychology mind games. She's genuinely tardy, as Laura often is; she just assumes that whoever's waiting will be patient and forgive her. All her friends have gotten used to it, considering themselves to be on "Laura time" when they're meeting her. Even I, for the most part, have adapted, but our spanking dates are special. I've made it clear that she's to treat them with the utmost importance and care, if she's truly dedicated to our play.

Merely because she wasn't late on purpose, though, doesn't mean she's above trying to tease me into going easy on her. She steps forward, pushing me until I relent and let her inside. Then her hand goes automatically to my cock. "Miss me?" she asks with a smirk as she massages my dick. The rules of our relationship are clear; I can spank her, and we can be naked together, but Evangeline doesn't want me touching her private parts, or her mine. While we've found ways to push the limits of those restrictions, I take care to abide by them, even though it's maddening sometimes to watch her pussy get wetter and wetter as I smack her ass and not be able to feel precisely what I'm doing to her.

I grab her hand and shove it behind her back. She's a feisty girl, and immediately tries to fight me, plunging us into a mock wrestling match I'm destined to win. "Aren't you even going to say you're sorry?" I ask, pinning her down so her hands are raised above her head, her cheeks flushed, her breathing heavy as she surrenders to my superior strength. I know that even that little bit of immobilization has her aching to be spanked—and fucked.

"Maybe," she says, her voice rising in the sexiest lilt I've ever heard. Even if she didn't have the slamming body and completely masochistic nature she does, her voice could do me in every time.

"'Maybe'? Oh, I think more like 'definitely.' I'm going to make you say you're sorry, girl. You were forty-five minutes late! I really should've left right away, and your punishment would've been to go home with your bottom as pale and bare as it is right now. But I'm going to make you pay, don't you worry," I say, my cock stiffening as I speak the stern words. She sticks her tongue out at me, but rolls over quite willingly when I let up on her arms and nudge her over. I decide to start off right there on the floor, pulling off her shoes and tossing them into a far corner, where they land with a thud.

"You're going to get forty-five whacks—one for every minute you were late. I know, you think that's nothing, but those won't all be with my hand, I'm not that dumb," I say as I push her skirt up. I yank off her fishnets, the tearing sound ringing pleasingly in my ears. Usually she gets totally naked, but her skirt is so short I can practically see her ass, and the image of the tiny garment shoved up above her lower curves, with her white cotton panties around her knees, is too hot to resist.

My dick is pressing upward against her stomach as she does her best to make me come in my pants, wiggling and squirming. I shove my fingers through her mass of sleek back hair and tug, watching her neck bend backward just so. I tug harder, just enough to make her body ripple in pleasure. "Stay still, Laura; you'll like this better. You're going to count for me, and if you mess up, we'll have to start over, but I know you won't mess up," I say somberly. She gazes back at me with a look that would wrecked a lesser man, her moist lips slightly open, her eyes wide and luminous, her nostrils flaring, her need to be spanked, by me, etched as strongly into her skin as a tattoo. Over the course of our relationship, I've figured out just what sets her off, and I know how to take her into that magical sub space with just the sound of my voice and a simple tug on her hair or snap of my fingers.

I let go of her hair, catching the gentlest of sighs pass from her lips. Her ass is right there, all mine for the taking, wide and round and pale and perfect. She's got just enough meat on her bones to make her rump perfect for spanking; girls who are too thin make me worry I might truly be hurting them, and I like asses that are wide enough to cover a range of smacks, ones where I need to hit them a few times to cover the entire cheek. I place my left hand on her lower back, letting my thumb graze the upper edge of her asshole. I'd love to press it against her sweet puckered hole, but I save that for Evangeline. With Laura, it's all about hinting, dancing around the edge of our desire, getting the most bang for our buck, if you will.

I press down against her body, ensuring that she won't jerk when the first blow lands. Then I raise my hand and bring it crashing down against her right cheek, hearing the boom, seeing her skin go from pale to pink in moments. "One, sir," she says, her voice loud and direct. It always starts off strong, as if she's trying to show me exactly how powerful she can be even spread across my lap. By the end, I'll have her whimpering out her numbers—if I'm doing my job right.

I roll her slightly forward to get the best angle, then do the same to her left cheek. "Two, sir," she responds dutifully. I keep going until ten, my palm stinging as the heat roars through our flesh. I pause there, rubbing my palm against her curves, ready to take things to the next level.

"Get up," I tell her, unceremoniously shoving her off me. My cock is pressing hard against my jeans, and I'm dying to whip it out and touch myself, even for a minute, but I know that could lead to dangerous territory. If her mouth goes anywhere near my dick, as besotted as I am with Evangeline, I might not be able to resist, so I keep it in my pants and work out my arousal another way. She gives me that look again, the one that silently begs for more, the one that tells me, without even looking, how turned on she is. "Bend over the bed," I tell her, and she hobbles up, knowing I don't mean for her to change any part of her attire.

Not only do I like to see her bent over, but I also know this means her piercings press against her sensitive nipples, arousing her further. Her skirt has flipped back down to caress the curves of her ass, so I push it back up, noting how already in a few minutes the redness in her cheeks has faded slightly. I pick up the belt, wrapping its sturdy leather around my hand, then running it across her cheeks, tapping lightly. "Hmmm," she moans, her head turned to the side, her eyes closed, as if lost in her own personal reverie. I need to snap her out of wherever she is right now and bring her back to me.

I push the belt to her lips, startling her eyes open. "Kiss it, then tell me what number's next," I demand.

Something breaks open inside me, swelling not only my cock but also my insides, puffing me up, when her lips purse immediately. She gives the belt a solid smack, then says in her most matter-of-fact tone, "Eleven, sir," as if telling me what she's made for dinner. Her eyes watch me, this time not so much begging as seeking, staring back at me as an equal partner in our game. She knows how much I like to spank her, and I know how badly she needs it, but both of us go along with this game anyway, adding to the thrill. Actually, making the thrill happen; without me on top and her below, spanking her would be no fun at all, something a machine could do quite as well.

"Get ready" is all I say as I move to the side so I can hover directly over her ass. Something about a woman's bottom makes it look even hotter when it's raised the way she has it, so round and firm and tempting, as if it was made with just such a kinky purpose, and no other, in mind. I let the belt whiz through the air once, its snap, crackle, and pop music to my ears. I strike the air again, right next to her ass, and she squeaks, a high-pitched noise that sounds as beautiful as any melody. Then I strike her for real, slashing the stripe of leather against her flesh, searing her skin in a way my hand simply cannot do. "Eleven," she chokes out in a robotic voice, as if it were not a number but the normal response when one has been struck dumb. The pain blooms instantly on her skin, a pretty line that makes me want to lean down and kiss it. Taking away her pain is almost as enticing as causing it, but we have thirty-four more whacks to go.

I let the belt lash against the area where her asscheeks meet her upper thighs, that never-never land of sensual flesh that is disproportionately tender. Like when I'm fucking and trying to hold off from coming, I have to think about something else for a moment besides the beauty of her welting curves, her *do-me* posture, her *have-me* stance, her *I'm-yours* body language. Sometimes I wonder if the constraints on our spanking dates aren't too much for either of us to bear. Evangeline has my heart, plain and simple, but my cock, my hands, my mouth, my power—those I would share with Laura, if I could. Instead, I must convey all that I want to do to her in these strokes, these beatings that take on so much more than their share of emotional energy.

She calls out the numbers as the belt slams against her ass, spreading her legs enough to give me a glimpse at what's between them. I haven't told her to, but I haven't told her not to, and for the moment, I let it go, too pleased with the slick pink shine I see there to argue. I drop the belt at twenty-five, then pick up the wooden paddle. I could insist on the blindfold, but I like the look on her face when she sees what I'm holding—half horror, half need. It's like the look Evangeline gets right before she comes, as if she's tempted to push me away, to stay teetering on the precipice instead of dropping over the waterfall's edge. I know my job is to urge her on, for the reward is always so much greater than the risk.

The pain lasts for only a few moments, her ass smarting, but the pleasure will keep Laura going for days. I hold the toy that resembles a Ping-Pong paddle, only thicker, with holes to let air through, then tilt my wrist and let it fly against her reddened cheek. "Twenty-six" comes out muffled as she absorbs the blow. I pause, trailing the backs of my fingers along her skin, then pinching a bit between my thumb and forefinger. I kneel down behind her and pull her cheeks apart, staring at the forbidden fruit of her pussy.

I need her to come, but I can't interrupt the flow of our play. I deliver the final blows with the black leather paddle, the simple yet stern one, its shiny surface too cheerful for the kind of sting it delivers. Her voice rises and falls as my arm does the same, until her ass rivals her lips in terms of redness, even after she's gnawed on her lower lip while taking her punishment.

If she were Evangeline, I'd simply pull down my zipper, get behind her, and shove my cock deep into her waiting hole. She'd convulse instantly around me, tears of joy filling her eyes but not spilling out, while I marveled at how her heat seemed to travel into my body. I'd try, but fail, to wait, and simply pump my hot lava into her tight tunnel, the explosion feeling truly volcanic. But she's Laura, my play partner, my standing spanking-date, my toy, even though she means no less to me where it counts.

Because it's she and not my girlfriend, I will wait to jerk off until she leaves. But she can't wait, and we both know it. "Lie down on your back," I order. It takes her a few seconds through the haze of arousal to get into position, but I let her have them, knowing that the crisp, clean sheets are rubbing against her sore ass. She goes to remove her panties, but I still her hand. "Keep them on," I say, sliding them down to her ankles and hearing the fabric strain and rip slightly. I don't care. I stand between her legs, holding her feet apart as she looks up at my towering presence, my erection practically undoing my zipper on its own. She used to be tentative, taking light swipes at her clit, not really indulging in her masturbation ritual until a good half hour had passed.

Now, she gets right into it, shoving three fingers deep inside while her other hand tweaks her nipples into tight, fierce points. "That's it, fuck yourself for me, Laura. That's your reward for taking your spanking like a good girl, even though you were late and had no excuse and are really a very bad girl to the core." I like to punish and reward her at the same time when I can, plant a seed of doubt (besides the obvious one) so that she'll give me some reason to keep on spanking her. "Picture my cock sliding into your mouth, right now, me climbing on top of you, your wrists tied above your head, your lips open and ready. Your friend Kira is fucking your pussy with a dildo at the same time, and I'm pinning you down with my dick so you can't move except to enjoy being filled in two holes at once." I know my words are getting to her, from the way she clenches her fingers, the way her face convulses, her eyes fluttering open to look at me, then shutting when the intensity gets to be too much. I wait, feeling triumphant when her climax seems to glide over her, making her curl up into herself. I let her go, let the panties slide off as she does what she needs to do. I'm absolutely turned on, but also wistful, wishing I could touch her and help take her to that higher place.

She gives me her panties as a present, a souvenir to sustain me until next time, a little secret for me to hide away, a compromise between my allegiance to Evangeline and my unquenchable need for Laura and her sweet ass. "So I'll see you next week, at six, right?" I ask as she steps into her gargantuan shoes, the height making her look older, wiser, but still as needful of a spanking. She nods and I grab her chin, holding her face and gaze steady. "Don't be late, or you may really get what's coming to you," I warn, trying to summon the proper vengeful tone. I can't quite get there, though, because no matter how late she is, I'll still want—no, make that *need*—to spank her, still lust after her and dream about her ass even when I have my girl's firm curves right before me.

And no matter what I use on Laura when she's bent over, no matter how firmly I plant my hand on her skin as she's asking for it harder and stronger, she knows who really holds the paddle in this relationship. She's got me exactly where she wants me—on top, looking down at her, my hand raised, my dick hard. And if you want to know the truth, there's nowhere else I'd rather be.

SCHOOLGIRL AND ANGEL

Thomas S. Roche

She stood there at the very edge of my swing space, watching with evident rapture and squirming her ass back and forth in her tight little schoolgirl's skirt. This section of the dungeon was brighter than the rest, because it's where the heavy punishment took place. Therefore, it was easy for me to see her in the long line of mirrors behind the St. Andrew's cross.

I've always bitched about those mirrors at The Sanctuary—an accident with a singletail could shatter one of them in an instant—but at the moment, I was happy they were there, if only because she looked so good in the skirt. The fact that she wasn't wearing anything but a skimpy white bra on top added to the pleasure of it. Her tits were magnificent, and the mesh bra was mostly see-through. Her nipples stood pink and erect through the thin fabric.

Her hair was black, obviously dyed. I could tell from the cut of her pretty face that she was well into the time of life when that hair was probably gray under its artificial coloring. She had the look of the early-forty-something latecomer to the dungeon—eyes wide and fascination obvious with everything she saw. I had watched her sauntering around the dungeon, turning down come-ons from an endless line of leather-clad Daddy types; despite this, her arousal was evident.

Perhaps a half hour ago she had brushed by me in the crowded dungeon, and the scent of her had been enough to make my cock hard in my blue jeans.

Angel was squirming, too, not least because of the hot line of stripes I was placing across her beautiful ass with my newest flogger. After a warm-up with my hands and the lightest flogger I had, she had counted to twelve, obediently, each time saying, "Thank you, Sir, may I have another?" which was her own particular turn-on, not mine.

She was reaching her limit, though. The reddening of her ass didn't tell me that, but the tug of her body against the chains of the St. Andrew's cross did.

"Just a little punishment," she'd told me, and I'd pursed my lips trying to hide my disappointment. With Angel, delicious as she is, "a little punishment" means half a spank and a minimal tweak of the nipples. Then, without fail, she was ready to fuck.

Now, as I laid on strokes thirteen, fourteen, and fifteen, she began to add "Ow!" and "Eeech!" sounds to every "Thank you, Sir," and I felt the pulse in my muscles that made me want to lay it on thicker—and the torture in my nice-guy soul that made me hold back.

Now, the older woman was creeping closer, leaning in to the bubble of play, invading my swing space in a way that I could hardly hold against her, since I kept inching back.

"Care to take a swing?" I asked her, turning and holding out the butt of the flogger. Angel and I had a curious kind of agreement—when she's tied up, anyone I wish can hit her, provided they don't hit her too hard.

The older woman gave the most girlish of giggles, hiding her pinkening face behind her hand. Her green eyes danced.

"Oh, God no," she said, her flirting obvious. "I could never hit another woman."

I smiled. "It's fun," I said.

Her eyes brightened slightly, a wicked smile playing across her red-painted lips.

"I'm sure she's having more fun than you are."

Angel had started to squirm some more, so I gave her three more blows in rapid succession without giving her a chance to thank me. She said "Ow! Ow! Ow!" emphatically rather than doing so, and I felt a rush of top's guilt.

I came up behind Angel, put my hand tenderly on her ass, feeling it squirm under my fingers.

"Too much?"

She shrugged, an odd gesture when one is strapped to a St. Andrew's cross. "Maybe I'm just not in the mood for a flogging. You mind?"

"Not at all," I said, reaching for the restraints. "Need a cool down?"

"Nah, I'm good," she said with a casualness that made it seem like I had asked if she wanted another beer.

"I'll let you down, then." I kissed Angel on the side of the neck.

"What's with Demi Moore?" whispered Angel when my face came close.

It took me a minute to figure out what she was talking about. There was no resemblance, really, but the woman in the schoolgirl outfit did have the sultry look of the over-forty sexpot. Angel is always making snarky comments about the older women in the scene—and since she's the same age as me, twenty-three, to her that's pretty much all of them.

I shrugged. Lips close to Angel's ear, I said, "I don't know. She's watching."

"So, ask her to play!" hissed Angel. "She's obviously into you!"

I glanced back at the schoolgirl, who was staring at us with big, wide eyes.

"I think she's into *you*," I said bitterly. With her bleached, close-cropped hair and pierced nipples, Angel's the one who invariably draws the ladies.

"Bullshit," Angel whispered. "She's *such* a bottom." I finished with Angel's wrists and bent down to unfasten her ankle restraints. When I came back up she turned, kissed me, and growled, "I'm going to have one of those apple fritters, and when I come back if she's not at the very least strapped to this fucking thing, if not polishing your knob, I'm going to be very unhappy."

I cocked my head down at her. "You serious?"

Angel looked over at the schoolgirl and smiled. The schoolgirl simply smiled back.

"Oh yeah," Angel said. "If ever a look said 'fuck me bow-legged,' that's the look. Just know I'll be watching. After the fritter."

Angel bent down and retrieved her thong from the base of the cross. She stepped into it, then walked away, glancing over her shoulder to wink at me.

Angel and I had drawn a small crowd, pressing close in a sea of leather and flesh. The schoolgirl was closest, the only one to break the bubble and be slightly inside the line of blue tape on the cheap industrial carpet.

I held up the flogger and gestured at the cross. "Ladies? Gentlemen? We have a free cross. Anyone? Anyone?"

No one stepped up or made a sound, except for a faint rustling as the spectators seemed to shrink back slightly.

All except the schoolgirl.

I have never been good with picking up strange women at play parties. In fact, if Angel wasn't a particularly aggressive woman, I probably would never get anywhere. But now, my heart pounding, I managed to make an inviting gesture to the schoolgirl. I raised my eyebrows at her; she only stared with those fiery green eyes.

"Whips? Chains? Carefully calculated agony? Sexual degradation before a slavering crowd?"

The schoolgirl giggled.

"Is that your pick-up line?"

"I'm afraid it's the best I can do," I said. "I'm not much of a flirt."

Her gaze slid like butter over my legs, my cock, my face, and then came down to rest hungrily on the flogger in my hand.

"Can you hit any harder than you hit her?"

I put my hand over my heart.

"It wounds me that you'd need to ask!"

"Mmmm," she said, moving toward the cross. "Then I'm game. I like it on the pussy, though—mind if I'm facing out?"

"Uh," I said. "S-sure. Uh...how hard?"

She giggled, covering her mouth with her hands in that coquettish gesture that made my cock shudder. Her eyes had lowered to the bulge in my jeans.

"As hard as that?" she asked, and we both knew what we meant.

"Not even close," I said. "But I can try. What's your name?" I asked.

"Oh, just call me Schoolgirl," she said. "Please tell me *your* name isn't 'Darkness Master' or 'Lord of Shadows.' "

I pursed my lips, feigning annoyance.

"It's Daddy," I said. "That is, if Schoolgirl's *your* real name."

"It most certainly is," she said, looking as offended as a woman in chains can look.

"Your real father must have been a real pervert, then."

"Yes, Daddy," she sighed.

She smoothly stepped out of the skirt. She folded it neatly and doffed her bra with the calculated elegance of a woman who knows her breasts are absolutely beyond glorious. They were, full and firm and capped by those nipples I'd been watching through the bra.

Underneath she had a white garter belt and stockings, which I'd already known, given that there wasn't much to that skirt. What I didn't know was that she'd been savvy enough to wear her lacy white panties on the outside of her garters, so it came away easily as she took off her skirt. She smiled at me and tossed me her underwear. I caught it in one hand and resisted the urge to bring it to my face; I didn't need to, because I could smell her on it, wet and sharp and horny.

She leaned back against the cross, legs spread, smiling at me as I draped her panties on a stray eyebolt on the edge of the cross.

As I looked her over, she spread her legs a little wider and got more comfortable on the cross. The posture suited her immensely well.

"Ready when you are, Daddy," she said.

Her pussy was shaved, the tattoo of a coiled snake striking downward to bite her clit.

I hadn't expected my ham-handed come-on to work. Angel, more turned on by imagining my potential exploits than I am, is always trying to push me at available-looking women. It never,

ever works—probably because my response is usually to turn red and hide behind her.

There was no Angel to hide behind now, and Schoolgirl wasn't leaving much to the imagination.

"All right, Daddy," she cooed. "Tie me up."

I was frozen for a minute, looking over that glorious body. I came toward her, reaching for the restraints.

This cross was leaned back at an inviting angle, requiring me to lean against her a little as I secured her wrists. Her breasts were against me, her nipples so hard I could feel them against my chest through the thin T-shirt I wore. I could also feel my cock pressing hard through my jeans, against her smooth belly. She squirmed a little against me, making my cock ache. I could smell her: the scent of a horny female body with a hint of shampoo, soap, something sufficiently feminine to remind me, in case there was any chance I'd forgotten, that this was a breathtakingly sexy woman I was strapping naked to a cross.

"You know, snakes don't strike downward," I said nervously, providing a fact that I'd completely made up.

"I hope *you* do," she said with a smile, her breath sweet in my face as I circled her wrist in the padded leather.

"Should we do all that safeword crap?"

"I've watched you," she said, and I felt my face flushing. "You can tell. Besides, 'safeword' works if it really gets down to it."

"You just want a flogging? On, er, on your pussy?"

I was leaning close enough that she could do it without much effort, the movement of her face to mine sure and confident. She planted her lips on mine and I tasted her tongue, felt the post through it grazing my lips.

"Oh, I want *so* much more than a flogging on my pussy, Daddy," she sighed when our lips came apart, a delicate filament of spit crackling between them. "But there's your pretty little girlfriend to consider."

I secured Schoolgirl's other wrist and shrugged. "She likes to share."

Schoolgirl giggled, this time unable to hide her mouth behind her hand.

"Then skip the flogging for now," she said with a wicked look.

I knelt down between her legs, the scent of her pussy sending a pulse through me as I secured first one ankle, then the other. I glanced up at her and had to fight the urge to press my mouth to her cunt, take a big hungry bite where the snake was striking. Her lips were slim and slight, but her clit was enormous, begging for attention. Erect, it almost reminded me of a crooked finger, summoning me in.

Her eyes were doing the same. I don't know if she nodded or I merely read the hunger there. But I was so fucking hard I wasn't thinking straight, and a top—*especially* a Daddy—must always, always think straight. Mustn't he?

My mouth descended between her legs hungrily, and I found her clit with my tongue. She let out a sudden, ecstatic moan of pleasure, and my pounding heart gave a flutter as she ground her body against mine, coaxing me deeper into her sex.

She was so wet that the flick of my tongue between her small, tight lips brought a bead of moisture leaking out and onto my chin. I licked deeper and she shuddered against the cross, pulling violently on her restraints as if completely out of control of her actions.

I drew back and looked up at her, feeling stupid for wondering if this was consent—a moan and a squirm and a shiver.

She met my gaze and said in a musical voice rich with sarcasm, loud enough for the spectators to hear: "Oh, no, Daddy. Not there. Don't lick me *there*—it's too dirty. Filthy, dirty,

Daddy—anything but that, *please,* Daddy!"

A vicious kind of arousal coursed through me, then, the kind that makes my stomach twirl and my heart beat like a jackhammer. And my cock got so hard that, as they say, it didn't have a conscience, even a conscience of the sex-positive, socially responsible kind.

I had never had any woman talk to me like that—not even Angel, after all-night discussions about how the hottest thing she could do was surprise me with how perverse she was. She was perverse, don't get me wrong—but she was not the verbal type.

I had the creepy feeling of being watched, and not only by the multitudes of strangers who had crowded around to see Schoolgirl on the cross. When I glanced over my shoulder, there was Angel, apple fritter in one hand, her other hand making an enthusiastic thumbs-up sign as she gave me a stage wink that would have done Eric Idle proud. Her tongue made an obscene thrust into the ripped-open guts of the custard-filled fritter, the slurp audible even across the play floor. Angel could be such a frat boy sometimes.

I looked up again and Schoolgirl looked down at me with hunger in her eyes, her mouth hanging slack in silent encouragement/enticement/approval. I brought my mouth to her cunt and hungrily began to work my tongue against her, savoring the cries she gave as I drew circles around her clit, suckled on it, caressed her inner thighs.

Her cunt held such inexplicable magnetism that I was a little surprised when I found my two fingers sliding easily into its tight embrace—and even more surprised when I heard Schoolgirl crying out and felt her grinding herself onto my hand, pushing my fingers deeper.

Her G-spot was swollen, full. I could feel its spongy curve against my fingertips and feel her whole body tense and shiver when I pressed firmly against it. I continued to tongue her clit, finger fucking her rhythmically in a come-hither gesture of my own, while my cock pulsed with every stroke.

"Fuck, Daddy," she gasped. "Where did you learn to do that?"

I took my mouth off her sex long enough to say, "Same place you learned to pick up strangers and call them Daddy—in the gutter."

I almost thought I saw her blush, but that didn't lessen her enthusiasm as I went back to licking her. Her juices dripped wetly down my hand and onto my arm, and her cries rose in pitch, her legs tensing.

She was going to come.

I'm not sure what made me stop—if, as a top, as a *Daddy,* I wasn't ready for my victim—my little girl—to come—or if the sudden power of my tongue and my fingers terrified me, this stranger's response too right, too perfect, for me to accept it into my brain.

I stood up, slipping my fingers out of her—I think I had it in my brain to ask her if she was all right, if this was all right, if it was okay to finger her and lick her clit and make her come. Which might seem stupid in retrospect, but this had all happened so fast I still didn't quite believe it was real.

A glance over my shoulder told me it wasn't Angel stopping me—on the contrary, she'd managed to drag over a nearby folding chair and was propped on it, legs spread, eyes wide, one hand pinching her own nipple, the other hand down her thong.

So I turned back to Schoolgirl, and leaned close to whisper something—anything—anything to break the tension, the overwhelming sense that if I didn't fuck her silly right then, right there.

When I came in close to her face she caught my mouth and kissed it, tongue sliding deep, as if hungry for my mouth, for her own juices. She ground her body against mine, her nipples rubbing firm, her body shaking against the chains.

"Can you fuck standing up?" she whispered, performing a deft motion to bring one thigh into contact with my cock.

"You asked me for a flogging," I said.

Then a delicate shiver went through her naked body, and the look in her eyes was enough to make me fuck her right there, against the slanted cross, with a roomful of perverts watching. If only it hadn't been for what she said next.

"Oh, no, Daddy," she said, voice shaking. "Not a flogging. Don't whip my thighs, Daddy, please—not my pussy, Daddy, please, *please* don't whip my pussy, anything but that!" Her voice was thick with desire.

My hand was already on my flogger. I stepped back, cock throbbing, eyes fixed on the cunt that still glistened with my spittle. I drew the flogger around in a big, easy circle, wishing I had a smaller one to start with—but not really caring.

The first blow struck her exposed cunt with a swish and a slap and another swish. It brought a thunderous moan from Schoolgirl's lips, and an echo-like "Oh, yeah," from behind me—Angel. She always did like watching other women get punished; she's not much of a masochist herself.

When I looked back, her hand was deeper in her thong than it had been before—and her eyes were on me, not my victim.

I brought the flogger around again, striking her cunt harder this time. She moaned louder, threw her head back, and groaned on the verge of a scream, and I hesitated with the next blow until I saw her head lowering, eyes meeting mine, and heard her moan, "Green, Daddy."

I hit her again, and she squirmed and trembled on the cross, gasping, whimpering. Again, and she all but went slack in her bonds, leaning hard against the cross. This time, she didn't say,

"Green," but rather, "Fuck me. Fuck me, Daddy."

I had that sudden sense of a person in my swing space, but by the time I looked around, Angel's hands were already around me from behind, her hands deftly working my belt. She had a condom tucked between her fingers, the wrapper already discarded. She got my cock out and stroked it slowly up and down, pinching the condom's head and smoothly rolling it down.

"If you don't fuck that schoolgirl right now," Angel growled, "I'll never forgive you. And neither will she."

Schoolgirl stretched on the cross, moaning, lifting her ass toward me, grinding her hips rhythmically. I dropped the flogger then, and lunged toward her, hearing her softly whimpered "Fuck me, Daddy," all but silenced by my mouth on hers.

My cockhead slipped easily between those small lips. She was even wetter than when I'd left her. My first thrust brought a deafening groan from her lips, her body so tight around my cock that I would have come immediately if not for the condom. I leaned heavily against her as I began to fuck her. My fingers pinched her nipples, softly at first and then harder as she choked out, "Yes, Daddy," and each thrust brought a louder moan—until she came, her muscles clenching my shaft, her body straining against the chains as she strove to fuck herself onto me, to meet every thrust with one of her own. As she came, she screamed my name, "Daddy!" so loud she all but deafened me.

But there weren't many more thrusts—because I was so fucking turned on that I came a moment later, grasping her long black hair and tangling it in my fist as I held my schoolgirl in place to kiss her, hard and deep, still tasting her cunt. When the strength went out of my thighs, she caught me neatly between hers, holding me up as I slumped against the cross and against her.

"Need a hand?" came a whisper from Angel as she reached

down between Schoolgirl's thighs and helped secure the condom while my cock slipped out of her.

"Did you train him?" sighed Schoolgirl as Angel leaned close.

Angel cocked her head at Schoolgirl.

"I mean...that's quite a tongue he's got. And quite a cock. Did you..."

Angel gave me that sarcastic look she's famous for. She shrugged.

"I'm sure nobody could ever train *him*," she said.

Schoolgirl's lips, all smeared red lipstick and the faintest hint of a smile, gave her own shrug, rattling the chains.

"I'm not so sure," said Schoolgirl. "Maybe it just takes two."

"Maybe," said Angel suspiciously, and, without asking, leaned in to kiss Schoolgirl, who not only didn't argue but moaned softly as their tongues met.

We got Schoolgirl down from the cross and took her home with us so fast we forgot her panties.

As it turned out, though, she didn't need them.

ABOUT THE AUTHORS

LEE ASH is a U.K. author who has published half a dozen erotic novels, novellas, and countless short stories, all firmly set within the genre of BDSM at its most punishing. He writes principally for the U.K. imprint Silver Moon and regularly contributes to the website Darker Pleasures.

M. CHRISTIAN is the author of the critically acclaimed and best-selling collections *Dirty Words, Speaking Parts,* and *The Bachelor Machine.* He is the editor of twenty anthologies, including *Amazons, Confessions,* and *Garden of the Perverse* (all with Sage Vivant), and *Blood Lust* (with Todd Gregory). His short fiction has appeared in over 200 publications, including *Best American Erotica, Best Gay Erotica, Best Lesbian Erotica, Best Transgendered Erotica, Best Fetish Erotica, Best Bondage Erotica,* and...well, you get the idea. His first novel, *Running Dry,* is available now from Alyson Books.

MATT CONKLIN is the pseudonym of an accomplished musician, writer, and craftsman. He is partnered with a devoted woman who is as interested in exploring the kinky nooks and crannies of her psyche as he is.

MACKENZIE CROSS is many things: author, educator, trainer, mentor, and visionary. Having discovered his dominant nature at an early age, he developed his unique style while training and mentoring submissive females through the years. Using his past experiences while looking to the future enables Cross to be innovative in his approach to education. One such endeavor he hopes to pursue is a school dedicated to the training of quality dominants as well as submissives.

ANDREA DALE lives in Southern California within scent of the ocean. Her stories have appeared in *Best Lesbian Erotica,* Fishnetmag.com, *Ultimate Undies,* and *The MILF Anthology,* among others. Under the name Sophie Mouette, she and her co-author saw the publication of their first novel, *Cat Scratch Fever,* in 2006 (Black Lace Books), and they have sold stories to *Sex on the Move, Sex in the Kitchen, Best Women's Erotica,* and more. In other incarnations, she is a published writer of fantasy and romance. Her website can be found at www.cyvarwydd.com.

AMANDA EARL is a Canadian writer of poetry and erotic fiction. Her erotica has been published in *The Mammoth Book of Best New Erotica 5.* Other anthologies that include her stories are *Cream: The Best of The Erotica Readers and Writers Association, The Mammoth Book of Best New Erotica 6,* and *Iridescence: Lovely Shades of Lesbian Erotica.*

SHANNA GERMAIN is a freelance writer based in Portland, Oregon. Her work has appeared in a wide variety of books, magazines, newspapers, and websites, including *Aqua Erotica, Best American Erotica 2007, Best Bondage Erotica 2, Caught Looking, Naughty Spanking Stories from A to Z 2,* and *Slave to Love.* When not writing erotica, she spends time teaching, traveling, and continually searching for that elusive grail, the perfect orgasm. You can read all about her online at www. shannagermain.com.

DEBRA HYDE avidly engages in many things sadomasochistic and stands particularly dedicated to her superior partner. Her fiction appears in many Cleis Press anthologies, the most recent of which are *Caught Looking: Erotic Tales of Voyeurs and Exhibitionists, Slave to Love: Sexy Tales of Erotic Restraint,* and *The Happy Birthday Book of Erotica.* Her S/M novel, *Inequities,* was published in 2006. Visit her at her blog, pursedlips.com.

MIKE KIMERA was raised as an Irish Catholic in England and now works as a management consultant in Switzerland. At the age of forty-three he started writing stories about sex and lust and the things they do to us; six years later, he's still at it. His work has been included in nine erotica anthologies. In 2005, *Writing Naked,* his first collection of short stories, was published. Its title story won the 2005 Rauxa Prize for Erotic Writing.

GWEN MASTERS has, over the last twelve years, written several novels, been featured in dozens of anthologies, and published hundreds of short stories. She has been featured in such gems as *Best American Erotica 2006* and the *Mammoth Book of Erotica 6.* She works as an editor for Clean Sheets and is a regular contributor to Ruthie's Club. For more information on her and her works, visit her website at www.gwenmasters.net.

N. T. MORLEY is the author of seventeen novels of erotic dominance and submission, most recently *The Dancer.* Morley's stories have also appeared in the *Naughty Stories from A to Z* series, the *Best New Erotica* series, and many other anthologies.

TERESA NOELLE ROBERTS writes erotica, poetry, romance, and speculative fiction. Her erotica has appeared in *Best Women's Erotica 2004, 2005,* and *2007, Secret Slaves: Erotic Stories of Bondage,* FishNetMag.com, and many other publications. She is also one-half of the erotica-writing duo Sophie Mouette, whose novel *Cat Scratch Fever* was released in 2006 by Black Lace Books. When not writing or copyediting, she can often be found belly dancing or enjoying the beach.

THOMAS S. ROCHE's short fiction has appeared in more than 300 magazines, websites, and anthologies, including the *Best American Erotica* series and the *Best New Erotica* series. He can be reached through his website, www.skidroche.com, or his weblog, thomasroche.livejournal.com.

JASON RUBIS lives in Washington, D.C. His fiction has appeared in many anthologies, including *Sacred Exchange, Erotic Fantastic, Leather, Lace, and Lust, Sexiest Soles: Erotic Stories About Feet and Shoes,* and *Secret Slaves: Erotic Stories of Bondage.* He is a staff writer at Custom Erotica Source (www.customeroticasource.com).

LISABET SARAI, some six years ago, experienced a serendipitous fusion of her love of writing and her fascination with sex. Since then she has published three erotic novels, including the classic *Raw Silk,* and coedited the anthology *Sacred Exchange,* a collection of fiction that explores the spiritual aspects of BDSM relationships. Her latest work, a highly praised collection of her short stories titled *Fire,* was released in 2005 by Blue Moon Books, and her erotic-noir novel, *Exposure,* was published by Orion in 2006. Sarai also reviews erotic books and films for the Erotica Readers and Writers Association (www.erotica-readers.com) and Sliptongue.com. She lives in Southeast Asia with her husband and felines. For more information on her and her writing, visit Lisabet Sarai's Fantasy Factory (www.lisabetsarai.com).

DONNA GEORGE STOREY enjoys saying "yes." Her fiction has appeared in Clean Sheets, Scarlet Letters, *Taboo: Forbidden Fantasies for Couples, Foreign Affairs: Erotic Travel Tales, Garden of the Perverse: Fairy Tales for Twisted Adults, Sexiest Soles: Erotic Stories About Feet and Shoes, Mammoth Book of Best New Erotica 4* and *5, Best Women's Erotica 2005* and *2006,* and *Best American Erotica 2006.* Read more of her work at www.DonnaGeorgeStorey.com.

ABOUT
THE EDITOR

RACHEL KRAMER BUSSEL is a prolific erotica writer, editor, journalist, and blogger. She serves as senior editor at *Penthouse Variations*, hosts the In the Flesh Erotic Reading Series, and wrote the popular Lusty Lady column for *The Village Voice*. Her books include *Naughty Spanking Stories from A to Z 1* and *2, First-Timers, Up All Night, Glamour-Girls: Femme/Femme Erotica, Ultimate Undies, Sexiest Soles: Erotic Stories About Feet and Shoes, Secret Slaves: Erotic Stories of Bondage, Second Skins, Caught Looking: Erotic Tales of Voyeurs and Exhibitionism,* and the companion volume to *He's on Top*, titled *She's on Top: Erotic Stories of Female Dominance and Male Submission.* Her novels *Everything But...* and *Eye Candy* are forthcoming from Bantam. Her writing has been published in over eighty anthologies, including *Best American Erotica 2004* and *2006*, as well as *AVN, Bust,* Cleansheets.com, *Diva, Girlfriends,* Mediabistro.com, *New York Post,* Oxygen.com, *Penthouse, Playgirl, Punk Planet, San Francisco Chronicle,* and *Zink.* Visit her at www.rachelkramerbussel.com.